close elsewhere

stories of translocation and whimsy

joshua kent bookman

LYS
Editorial office: redaktion@lysforlag.com
www.lysforlag.com
Editor: Sofi Tegsveden Deveaux
Book design: Andy Bolton

No part of this publication may be reproduced or distributed in any form or by any means, or stored in a database or retrieval system, without the prior written permission by the publisher.

Copyright © 2019 Joshua Kent Bookman & LYS läromedel
ISBN 978-91-985057-3-3

close to elsewhere

stories of translocation and whimsy

joshua kent bookman

preface by the editor
sofi tegsveden deveaux

The French word for weather, *le temps*, also means time. Weathering, unlike seasons, records years as linear. It imitates life; it is one-directional and with a definite closure. Storms and days of blasting sunshine form the landmarks that help us navigate our personal histories. It also adds meaning to space. Without light or weather, we hold only the architect's blueprint, eternal and uninhabited. The photograph, on the other hand, is that of experience and memory, momentary and forever in the past. And this is why we keep photographs, not floor plans, in our attempts to preserve what is no longer present. The migrant will not grieve the coordinates of her point of departure, but the sweet smell of mirabelle plums ripening along paths shaped by her feet. It is a scent of jam boiling unseen behind shutters that will transport her across continents and decades of estrangement, as she's hurrying down a street made for cars and buses.

The migrant should never be mistaken for a nomad. Homeless by circumstances, sedentary by nature, she seeks a fixed point in space, anchored to a future point in time. The passing of time marks her loss; there is another August passing with supermarket-branded jam, too sweet and not sweet enough. September offers what she knows as an October storm, gashing her makeshift shelter. But. There is also that sense of adventure, when the tears on her cheeks are just a little ocean water. There is that flash of unexpected November sunshine, or an improvised meal in the company of good strangers. There is that first bite into an exotic fruit, a celebration of new soil.

The map she carries is topographical and political, one of obstacles and borders, but her memories are that of her senses.

The traveller shares her experience. Regardless if he labels himself as a tourist, backpacker or explorer, his quest is that of weathers. By temporarily abandoning his everyday life for another, he expects to be impressed. His dreams of Cambodia are not of its people, government, agriculture or means of livelihood, but of a deep shade of yellow with a laxative effect.

Why are we so short on seeing this parallel? Why do we romanticize only those journeys that end where they begin? Are we scared of banalising the traumatic, suggesting joy in tragedy? Are we reluctant to admit that we are not that far from being one of them, the migrants? Are we cautious to bring up our own past, where, at some point between now and twelve thousand years ago, we were left without land or sense of belonging?

I am writing this from a desk in the old town of Stockholm — Gamla stan, in a building dating back to the 15th century. My screen reflects the window behind me. If I turn and reach out, my fingertips touch the facing window across the alley. Below, cobble stones, melting ice. This part of town was the first to be built and inhabited, and the first to become a museum showcasing itself. Being a conserved landscape, change is minimal and imitary. This way, such an environment is immune to settlers breaking ground. Locals shun its permanence, but for those in transit, surface makes sense.

On the short walk to the metro station, I am a stranger, too. I am surrounded by sounds, smells and languages that are all foreign to me. The mandatory souvenir shops display the usual mass-produced items, cementing and mocking the idea of local practice. People without names linger, tracing the same routes on the same tourist maps, pursuing the same hashtags on Instagram. If it wasn't for the symptomatic sleet of March, I could be anywhere.

On a global scale, the Swedish capital is ridiculously small, almost provincial. Plotted on a number of islands surrounded by brackish water and evergreens, it struggles to find a city vibe on its own, celebrating instead imitations of elsewhere: 'Stockholm's Manhattan', 'SoFo' and 'Venice of the North' are all established labels. Landmarks are modest and visions realistic. Still, it makes an attractive destination for tourists and migrants alike. The former are welcomed, the latter makes up a charged topic.

Recent figures state that 16% of the Swedish population are foreign-born, and the last decade has seen an influx of hundreds of thousands seeking asylum. The political agenda has narrowed this topic to one of legal, logistical and ideological dilemmas. We feel entitled to *opinionate* and to categorise the migrant. In the eyes of permanent resident, the migrant is either legible or illegible, child or adult, grateful or ungrateful, good or bad. If she is not one of us, she is one of them.

But this has not always been the case. *The Emigrants* (beg. 1949), a novel series by Swedish author Vilhelm Moberg, reminds of a time when roles were reversed. From the 1850's until the 1920's, almost one million Swedes left their native country for America. As many of these, the main characters of The Emigrants, Oskar and Kristina, leave their modest farm for Minnesota — a carefully selected destination due to it topographical and climatic reminiscence to rural Sweden. The price for a better life is, of course, hard and full of hardship; it is not until her death bed that Kristina gets to taste the first fruit from her Astrachan apple tree that she has planted with seeds brought from her home in Småland.

Selma Lagerlöf, too, addresses a complicated relationship to land and purpose in *Jerusalem* (1901), where a group of farmers embark on a long and seemingly impossible journey from the Swedish province of Dalarna to the land of Christ. Their intention is to never come back, sacrificing the worldly and their loved ones. Travelling by boat, their expedition was ambitious and risky, and the book tells of failure, regret and loss, all instigated by vanity. Eventually, however, the Nordic forests lure the protagonists back. As usual, disappointment is coupled with relief and the sorrow for everything that cannot be mended.

What can we learn from these literary precedents? What experiences are still relevant today? Migrant routes may be reversed and so also the landscape of opportunities, but feelings must stem from the same register.

Twelve months ago, I was invited to comment on the first tentative words looking for a story. Across that same Atlantic crossed by more than 30 million Europeans, Joshua Kent Bookman had begun the exploration of the migrant experience as represented in literature. By borrowing moments and trajectories from Swedish-, Bengali-, Italian- and American writers and their take on the translocational experience, he gave them new life and relevance. Paths were crossed, glances exchanged, recipes re-invented. Like me, Bookman was reminded of his own past, his colonist American origin, that is, migrary per definition, entitled by policy.

Integrating accounts, characters and conditions from these literary pieces, he frames the contemporary in the atemporal, mapping fragments of narratives that repeat and mirror themselves, across continents, over centuries. But this is no geographical cartography, but one of relationships and memory. Like Nils in *The Wonderful Adventures* (Selma Lagerlöf, 1906), we are invited to explore the concept of scale, through the vantage point of fiction. Parallel to this tale of family and land, Bookman has devised a legend that should not be overlooked; it holds clues on how to read terrain also elsewhere.

Food is a central theme to Bookman and his characters. Whereas the traveller seeks the new and exotic, the migrant chases ingredients that cannot be found. She tracks down substitutes, invents variants and grieves compromise. There is a celebration of the new, coupled with the resignation to availability. She adapts and re-invents her recipes, as per local conditions and climate. With that, there is a strong spatial dimension to nutrition, being perhaps the most intimate relationship between the human body and its immediate environment. The animalistic nature of this condition for life is perhaps the trigger for elaboration, turning iningestion into art, something human. Recipes, hacks and traditions are all passed down generations, secrets are kept and shared, seasonings discussed and dissected. As the traveller and migrant both know, flavour and smell are closely associated with place and time.

close to elsewhere was, like the Thomi's memories, drafted between geographies, with Bookman intermittently based in Los Angeles, Boston and a French vineyard. We were not only collaborating across time zones but also according to different measures of time. Behind Bookman's screen were the blazing wildfires of California, the echoes of French church bells, reports from a sleepy art gallery, children's distant voices from a tennis court. That is a world spinning faster than mine, that is accessible to me only in the his writings: red mud on tennis shoes, the dark swirls of wine being thrown out an open door, cracked leather on a bus, *going somewhere.*

I never met Josh in person. Still his face, although sometimes pixelated, is familiar to me. His voice, although often delayed or with an echo, is that of a friend. His dedication to flavours, smells and textures is uncannily intimate. Any remaining gaps are trivial. These are blanks that I can fill in on my own, making him part invented, fully real. It would be tempting to praise technology but technology is just a means. I praise humanity, language, fiction.

x

contents

v   preface by the editor

xiii   family tree

3   *one*   *1980 – Aquitaine; France*
                            2015 – New England; USA

21   *two*   *1955 – Liguria; Italy*

31   *three*   *1957 – Aquitaine; France*
                            1957 – Lazio, Liguria, Tuscany; Italy
                            1957 – Stockholm, Bohuslän; Sweden

67   *four*   *2014 – Alto Adige; Italy*
                            2015 – New England, California; USA

97   *five*   *1959, 2002, 2015 – New England; USA*

107   *six*   *2015 – New England; USA*

149   legend

155   glossary of experimental language

165   acknowledgements

167   about the author

family tree

L'ARBRE GÉNÉALOGIQUE

MONTALE (née 1935)   m.   MACAL (né 1930)
 Vita   Joel
                       |
    MONTALE (née 1960)   m. KEIGHLEY (né 1962)
     Elisa   Kirk
                       |
            KEIGHLEY (né 1995)
              Luca

one

*1980
Aquitaine; France*

*2015
New England; USA*

I
the process of bringing one's pieces into play

"*Zut!*" she cried.

In 1954 a sunrise was opening and slamming. So said a Swedish poet.

Luca thought of the line in another context. Boston 2015. It described the Monday after his long holiday.

"*T'as broughté quoi, maman*[1]?" Luca shouted.

From the hallway Luca had heard his mother open the garage door. He stopped to peek outside. Elisa was carrying two bags, spilling slightly as she tipped them over the kitchen counter.

"Some lemon ice," she said.

Luca darted to the kitchen and looked at Elisa. Both their eyes were piercing blue, their little secret kept in skylight.

"What if we add chili powder this time?" she asked, unsure, but daring.

Elisa dusted the ice with burnt orange.

"Oh my God," Elisa said.

"Yeah that's it," Luca said, sea salt added to his lips.

---

1 – mom what'd you bring (Franglais)

II
circumstances that form the setting

Before Elisa had opened her garage, she had been driving on the side streets near the house. She was daydreaming.

She was ambling along the coast of Cape Cod, pretending to be one of those hot air balloons, dangling a camera from the wicker basket. She was the camera. Squinting, zooming in, she could see chips of dark blue. Mussel shells were perched into the sand.

Elisa picked one of them up. The air was hazy but the mussel shell sparkled. She rotated it in her hand, her fingers chafing against barnacles. Ocean water flowed up her legs. Sea foamed.

Kelp strands clung to her body. Redder types of seaweed were also strewn across the shoreline, and had joined in, wrapping her toes, her ankles, nudging her to stand still.

III
baladant (n.) someone who gets lost to find an order of nature, derived from the French se balader, 'to saunter, to amble'

Far from that shoreline, an Aquitaine village defines work and observation differently. At the sun's zenith, roof tiles sit against the vines like stage lights.

September heat, 1980. The morning is busy for the weeks arriving, and the harvest of a whole year's anticipation.

The timeline is foreign to those not living there, like anyone not familiar with a rhythm three or more thunderclaps from their environment.

People there can wake up to cups of coffee, espresso puddling outwards as biscuits dip in, the aromas lifting upwards into quiet noses.

But someone decides to delay breakfast for a run, one last sprint through the vines, where stone houses watch onlookers volt past, rusticity that charges the off-paths, dirt roads split from side roads, the countryside further fractals, where a man named Thomi searches for meaning across time zones.

IV
from a particular place

For years Thomi would live between geographies. He'd be on the subway in Boston, but his mind would go to Bordeaux. Or he'd travel back home, and still think he was passing Fenway. A side street, dim 3 o'clock sunshine — some detail would make him think of the other city.

It would look like he was staring out into the distance, and he would just say he was thinking about something. He was always thinking so much and wouldn't tell anyone why.

Lately he had more trouble than usual in focusing.

"The view's crazy," Luca said. Thomi had hired the kid, a favor for his mother.

Luca was standing on naked wood, the second floor of what would be a patio. Him and Thomi were building a forest bar, a dream of the Frenchman ever since he had emigrated to the United States.

"You think this is beautiful, ha!" Thomi said, wrapping a scarf around Luca's head. "A shame then you don't know grandmother."

"Whose grandmother?" Luca asked.

"My grandmother," Thomi said. "No, I'm joking, yes."

"Okay, my grandmother, since well, you're insane," Luca said. "What do you mean I don't know her?"

IV

"Phff," Thomi said, a kind of whistle noise he'd make when he was debating how to spin something in his favor.

"She's like a myth," Thomi said.

Luca didn't move. He was waiting for Thomi to continue.

"She's…" Thomi said. "She's not exactly easy to know. Your mom doesn't like to reveal too much, so… so I do."

In that moment Luca stood, unflinching, staring at Thomi in the same way Elisa would. There was something honest in Luca's and Elisa's gazes that said they never meant to hurt anyone, even if they were hurting themselves in the process. Thomi liked that about their family, passing on to each generation an aloofness he was jealous of.

V

(in paleoclimatology) a period of time marked by a characteristic climate

"Snowtime!" Thomi shouted.

A large sack of flour smacked Luca right in the face. White plastered him.

"*Ratatiné*[1]," Thomi giggled. He flicked off some flour that had hit him.

Luca thought a summer helping Thomi would be a good use of freedom. That was a poor thought. He was dead man floating as a baker, drunk from overtime and the humidity.

"What the hell Thomi?" Luca said.

"I didn't do that, *non*[2]!" Thomi said. He had a purple polkadotted bandana wrapped around his head, the whiff of a lemon tart glazing him as he strutted, ostrich-like.

Luca wiped flour off of his apron. "If voodoo hour is over, can you take out the elephant ears?"

Thomi dropped his grin. He stared right at Luca.

"It's palmiers," Thomi said.

Thomi blew on his hands as if signaling his exit to the alleyway.

---

1 – smashed (French)

2 – no. A negation at the end of a sentence has a tendency to mean yes (French)

V

He looked at his assistant, and could see nothing more than spitshine polish.

"*Débrouille-toi* [3]."

---

[3] – fend for yourself (French)

VI
because in French the word for winemaker includes the imagery of a vineyard

Outside, Thomi could only focus on the brick.

"Elephant ears." The language was too simple. Luca was insulting the delicacy of French, he was bastardising sound so personal to Thomi that everything turned into a piss-off point.

It was stupid brick, stupid like all the other pastry names he had to relearn in America. He thought brownstone wasn't a very creative addition to the English language and just like that Boston's red-brown stonework became a flashpoint. Its clay and concrete composition conflagrated into memories of Bordeaux's architecture. The limestone buildings there were not constructed as he knew it here.

They were pale brown.

VII
in Burgundy, vigneron, or 'vine grower'

Thomi was living between geographies again. His mind wandered from the image of the city centre, following the pale brown buildings into a famous bookstore. It was painted a solid wood blue.

Every year he goes through this sequence to remind himself how he used to organize himself.

There is the wine and gastronomy section, the foreign literature, the books of art, music, film, philosophy, spirituality, history, the *bandes dessinées*[1]. He likes mistranslating that sense into English, the design of bands.

The "selected French literature" section has books with portraits and landscapes on the covers. Even the copies of pulp fiction feature hand-drawn illustrations.

He admires the inscriptions, the little notes with a paperclip that say "sensibility!" or "*coup de coeur*[2]." Again he translates poorly and imaginatively —

"A hit of the heart," the store says.

Thomi looks down, putting his hand on his chest, as if reciting the American anthem.

---

1 – comic strips (French)
2 – a favorite (French)

VIII
place over person

Thomi walked up to the bar's top deck. He saw Luca.

"Pretty view, right?" Thomi said.

Luca peered out from the top deck. Lichen covered a tennis court.

"It looks old," Luca said.

Thomi looked down and thought, it was only years ago he wasn't here. He remembered his time in that Aquitaine village, and thought the lichen here was pretty. Its teal color cracked through thick 'paque lines of white paint. The net drooped.

Without France, it should be a sad image.

"You're taking a little tan at least, *non*," Thomi said.

Sunlight flickered in-between nap sighs of the afternoon, and he imagined his feet sinking into the moss.

"Haha, yeah," Luca said, rubbing his elbow, embarrassed. The sun bleached his arm hair.

The Frenchman knew something Luca didn't. Thomi began to remember what he used to see, a landscape impacted by optimism.

This isn't decay, Thomi thought. This is a very noble rot.

IX
an alcoholic drink taken before a meal to stimulate the appetite

Thomi and Luca were hunched over milk crates in the pantry, gnawing on six-o'clock baguettes. Luca had overcooked them.

"Ehi *Legnosacro*[1]," Thomi interrupted. He liked to tease him with a college-stylized Italian, knowing Luca had ambitions to pursue.

"What do you want," Luca replied. He knew Thomi had yet another idea.

"What if we had a little wine bar in here," Thomi said. "You know, a glass and a bite. We could make some more... dough." He laughed at his own joke and then frowned. Money was his new homeland.

"Don't you mean an *aperitivo*[2]?" Luca asked.

"*Aperitif*[3]," Thomi said. He was domesticating Luca's way of speaking.

"*Aperitivo*," Luca said.

"Tif," Thomi said. Pretentious froufrou, that's what Luca was.

"Teeth," Luca said, pointing at his mouth.

"*Baguette de la merde*[4]," Thomi said, pointing at his teeth.

---

1 – sacred wood, translated into Italian as *legno sacro*

2 – pre-dinner drink (Italian spelling)

3 – pre-dinner drink (French spelling)

4 – shitty baguette (French)

X
typically a large structure

Elisa had not intended to daydream. She was driving to see the construction taking place, set on finalising financial arrangements with Thomi.

She parked the car only to hear him arguing with Luca. She tried to listen, but the wind kept laughing. All she could see was Luca and Thomi with their fingers in their mouths.

"Jean and Jacques, productive!" Elisa shouted. She liked to tease them as being two of the four 1930's tennis musketeers.

Luca shot his mother a look of embarrassment, leaving to avoid ridicule. Thomi remained where he was, three stories above her.

"So you can do it?" Elisa asked.

Thomi stood like a watchman, staring down to Elisa, smoking a cigarette. He tapped ash onto the forest floor, aiming to hit her feet.

"No," he said.

Thomi didn't want to lie about their history any more.

"What else would it take, c'mon," she said. He kept it airy; she wanted something more durable. But she knew Thomi could be manipulated.

Thomi bit one of his fingernails. Elisa stared at him, the blackness of her pupils piercing him. She was attractive, yes, he would admit.

15

X

He dropped a jagged piece onto the would-be entrance.

"Human in space," he said. "Like ocean dust."

"I'd prefer it if you weren't so existential," she said. Elisa thought he was drifting back to Bordeaux, or at least its outdated philosophies.

"The forest stays," he said, then pointing towards Luca. "He stays." "You stay."

XI
the quality in a person or society that arises from a concern for what is regarded as excellent in arts, letters, manners, scholarly pursuits, etc.

"I should've just double kissed him," Luca said. He was in the bar painting with Thomi.

He was explaining to Thomi that he didn't know his mother's cousin, so a hug wasn't appropriate, but neither was a handshake — it was too formal.

"*Non*," Thomi said. He shook his finger.

"Do you always say '*non*'?" Luca asked.

Thomi thought Luca was bad at paying attention. He didn't say *non* to Elisa.

"You say *pardon*," Thomi said.

"*Pardon*," Luca said.

"*Pardon*," Thomi repeated.

"No double kiss?" Luca asked.

"*Pas d*'double kiss[1]" Thomi said.

"Well how do men..." Luca said.

Thomi blew fake smoke towards him.

"Ask the Italians," Thomi said.

---

1 – no double kiss (*Franglais*)

XI

"That's your answer for everything," Luca said.

"Phff, *non*," Thomi said. "That's my answer for *everybigthing* you ask me. Not so simple to explain your lack of *formation*[2]."

Luca stared at him, his blank expression mimicking Elisa's.

Thomi blew a kiss. "Pardon, lack of upbringing. Try traveling for once, hm? Maybe you will see I am the good guy in this, the best guy you'll ever work for. Internship this, internship that, *non*! I will be the best character you see. You see, ha! I repeated myself!" Thomi was now cackling.

---

2 – education, but has an added sentiment of training, or specific preparation, particularly compared to a generalised liberal arts education in the United States (French)

two

*1955
Liguria; Italy*

XII
late 17th century (originally in the sense 'shake, toss'): from Middle Dutch *hutselen*. Sense 3 of the verb dates from the early 20th century

Zufo picked up the cups people left at the table, quickly bussing the silverware and the plates, but leaving the drinks in his archeryesque hands, dextrous, precise, pressing his fingers just so against the porcelain. He wanted to feel the warmth of the coffee. Tourists ran through the coast, hurrying up a "check please" to chase the next image they would frame, so he took it upon himself to slow down their morning. They had missed something in their mad dash to explore. Heat had left espresso rims.

"Y'also forgot the sugar packets!" he shouted towards wherever they had hurried off to, grinning just slightly. He thought the little crests on them were pretty, blue shields adorned with gold hatchets. The crests made the sugar inside feel like royal sweet crystals of the ocean.

"Made in America," Giulia said. Her eyes, the color of green sea glass, cut through to the heart of anyone she spoke to.

She took a packet from him, ripped it quickly and dunked the sugar into her mouth.

Vita was watching from the entrance. Her hair was frayed. She wore an apron that had the stench of the dumpster. She wasn't laughing. She was at the restaurant to work whereas Zufo taunted them with his laziness. He was still looking at the espresso cups.

They worked near ragged cliffs and exquisite water. The sea past itself was ocean. People said Zufo's eyes looked like the ocean color

XII

off the Adriatic and he always laughed. He didn't like to associate beauty with clichéd landscapes.

"Eho Vita what you looking at?" Giulia asked.

"Zufo," Vita said.

Zufo blushed. He rubbed his finger against the dried espresso, melting it into the table.

"A tourist walks in he asks for a menu what do you do?" Giulia said.

"*Salve*[1]! How about the pasta?" Vita said.

"No you say hello, talk about the weather... '*Signore*[2] what a beautiful day out how about a coffee!'" Giulia said.

"But if he's famished," Vita protested.

"Then pour a half glass of Vermentino with a little water and smile as you point towards the boats," Giulia said.

"There are no boats," Vita said.

"And there are no benefits to your twit of an attitude," Giulia said.

"But who helped me make it, eh?" Giulia continued.

Giulia slipped from her mind what she has always imagined.

Vita kept silent.

Giulia stared at one of the iron benches that skirted along the coast, beyond the bar. It was warped and dirty, she thought it was ugly and thought that God she was just sitting on that bench when she felt the back of her skirt covered in a tarish residue.

The sun felt hotter

"Someone pour me some of that wine!" Giulia shouted.

"Okay, okay," Zufo said. "Relax."

---

1 – hello (formal Italian)

2 – sir (Italian)

XII

"Don't tell me what to do," Giulia said.

"I'm making a suggestion, that's all. Ehi, you ever notice the coffee—"

"Zufo, shut up," Giulia said. "Yeah, I know. They never finish their coffee."

"Giulia, oh Giulia," Zufo said, shaking his head. "You really want some? I'll get you some good Vermentino."

"No, I don't want any," Giulia said.

"Nah, my treat," Zufo said. "We'll go to the bar later, after our shifts finish." Zufo saw the shock on Giulia's face. "No, not a date," Zufo said.

"Can I come too?" Vita asked.

"Not a date," Zufo said. "Yeah, we'll all go, c'mon Giulia." He wrapped an arm around her and kissed her on the cheek, seeing Vita in the corner of his eye, seating another set of sightseers, watching her ask them if they'd like a cup of coffee, them saying yes, closing their menus, sharing a tourist's kiss.

XIII
to remove (dirty) tableware in a restaurant or cafeteria

That morning Giulia had one puff of a cigarette. She didn't shower. Her hair was dry. She rushed outside and saw her bus leaving.

"Stop!" she shouted, two hair clips between her teeth. She spat them out on the side of the road.

"Stop!" her hand upright.

The two kids in the back window saw her, faces pressed against the glass. They disappeared.

The bus slowed to a loud rubber halt. She darted up to the front door. The bus driver nodded.

"Thank you," she said.

Giulia worked her way to an empty row and as she sat she breathed.

The cracked leather of buses relaxed her. She'd sweep her hand across her seat, feeling the warmth from the sunlight, and the grooves, created from disrepair. As she kept her hand there, she looked outside. Every couple of minutes the bus would get too close to the side of the road and small branches would scrape across the windows.

"Ehi, Giulia," Zufo whispered. He was waving at her. As he passed by her aisle, she felt the morning light against her face and closed her eyes.

XIII

Giulia traced the length of each cracked leather line, running her fingernails along the groove, wondering if she'd ever be someone different, stopping only to hear the window drums.

XIV
a temporary stop in action or speech

When Giulia got off the bus, she didn't immediately check in to work.

She walked towards the bus station's bike rack. She leaned against a bike, thinking she was going to smoke, but she didn't.

She stared at the bench next to her. It was mossy, a teal-colored lichen growing in no apparent pattern. It had a small plaque "1937–." There was no name, no inscription besides the date.

The bench shared a space with a willow tree.

There was also a pile of stones. Kids were sitting on them, elbows akimbo, prodding, joking at each other.

Giulia looked down at her bus ticket. It was a multicolored thickish paper — faded green and red, some sparkled gold. The paper felt like the roses people kept in old diaries. She stuffed it into her pocket.

An older man sat down at the bench. She wasn't sure how old he was, but she could see the deep purple squiggles on his legs, and the silver color of his hair. He had a chronograph resting on his kneecap.

Another bus arrived into the station.

XV
a seat for several people

The man on the bench had friends. He didn't think of this directly. He'd stare at the dirt. There were ants circling bits of grass. One of the ants drifted off, and ambled his way to a chipped pinecone. He found it strange that a pinecone could be chipped. He leaned his finger forward, gesturing towards the ant. It lifted its head.

The ant crawled slowly around the man's hand, circling the grooves of cracked skin.

A ridge of the pinecone could be seen far off into the distance. It was laying on another bench. It was sunbathing, enveloped in sun. A ruby-throated hummingbird swooped in and landed one foot onto the pinecone. The bird hovered, its tail extended out for balance.

He was going to ask Giulia if she was enjoying the sun, but she had so quickly rushed off he pretended the conversation.

"Good morning," he said.

"Hi," she said. She turned towards her side of the bench.

"What do you see on that bench over there?"

"What?" she said.

"Do you see that bird?"

The bird fluttered away as soon as she turned her head towards it.

"I'm sorry… I don't know what you're talking about," she said.

XV

"It's ok," he said. He shook his knees up and down a couple times.

Giulia looked at him. She felt bad. She thought he was lonely.

"What do you see?" she said, grabbing for her pocketbook. She lit a cigarette.

He hesitated.

"I see another bench past it."

She didn't understand.

"You see another bench," she said.

"Yes," he said. "There's a couple of kids over there. They're repainting it purple. It looks like the Bordeaux sky in April, a pale rain purple. Isn't that nice?" he said.

She looked over to the group of high school students. They were using little brushes at this point — you could barely see what they were detailing. She imagined they were painting willowisps.

"It's beautiful," she said.

"Yeah," he said, imagining a dance course he was attending that evening. It was his first class.

He didn't care to tell Giulia that most of his friends had died a long time ago. He had made new friends.

three

1957
Aquitaine; France

1957
Lazio, Liguria, Tuscany; Italy

1957
Stockholm, Bohuslän; Sweden

XVI
at or to the further side of

Vita had a couple weeks off from the restaurant. She decided to travel.

"Bordeaux," her mother said. "Are you sure?" They were in her bedroom. It was nighttime.

"No, I'm not sure," Vita replied.

"You don't know anyone there," her mother shot back.

"What's the risk of something random?" Vita asked.

Her mother was quiet, her eyes a bit watery. At night Vita couldn't see this.

XVII
a sailing vessel with a bowsprit and three or more square-rigged masts

Vita was on a ship. The wood was distressed, or splintered, she couldn't tell. Nails stuck out of the boards, sailors too busy flirting with the wealthy.

The wind submerged her. It felt like the cold water of the lakes she used to swim in.

She faced the wind head on because elsewhere was crowded. She saw one sailor, laughing with a pearl-necklaced woman. The top deck she couldn't afford.

"Brilliant day," he said. A young man had appeared next to her, maybe her age, but with his scratchy beard she couldn't tell.

Vita wrapped her scarf tighter around her neck.

"For me, yes," she said.

He raised his left eyebrow, surprised.

She laughed. She hadn't noticed until that moment his hair was orange.

"That's funny to you," he said.

"You're pretty," she said.

He turned pale and his eyes glowed. She turned pale as well.

"No that's not what I meant," she said, stuffing her fists in her coat pockets.

XVII

"Whatcha mean?" he said.

"Where I'm from you're new art," she said.

"What're ya a museum curator," he said, his accent thickening.

"No, no," she said, covering her mouth with her scarf.

"An art critic," he said.

She shook her head.

"A bird watcher," he said.

She paused. "You're not wrong," she said.

"What brings you here?" he asked.

"The wind," she said.

"America?" he asked.

She kept quiet, refusing to answer. He walked closer to her. She did not move.

"The wind's nice," he said.

He turned to Vita and again raised an eyebrow. "Is this where you birdwatch?" he said.

XVIII
journey along or through

The market on the *quai*[1] of the Garonne was like her mother's. There was the zucchini vendor, an apron worker, a selection of cheeses. But the champagne was new.

"Would you like to try?" a woman asked. She pointed at the plates of oysters.

Vita turned her head to the tables of market goers. A couple was sipping back shells, relaxing, grocery bags of bread and tomatoes sunburnt against the thin flutes of sparkling wine.

"Yes, just three please," Vita said. "And a glass if you would be so kind."

"Oh stop being so polite," the woman said.

A breeze flirted across the river as more people passed through the market. Vita became one of them, standing with her champagne and grocery bag, searching for an open table.

---

1 – quay (French)

XIX
a parcel within a vineyard that has its own terroir, or complete environment

The pale blues of the market drifted along, until it was foggy. Not from the weather, but from the mirror of water that would be there decades later, like a cut from Turrell's light spaces.

Children were splashing in it, adults too.

The sun was very warm, even in the fog. Vita didn't need sunglasses. She just sat there, admiring the histories of the city, looking at the sculptures on the buildings, the stone faces of slaves from two hundred years past.

A little boy walked past her, holding his father's hand, dragging a wooden racquet against the ground, bumps of sound every time the boy tried to lift the handle. His tennis shoes had red clay besprinkled on its soles, an impression, a temporary impression, that him and his father had just left the tennis club on the outskirts of the city, a club that would reach its centennial mark well after the boy and his footsteps had disappeared from the clay.

XX
a counteracting force

Vita appeared in Sweden. She walked along a trail into the deeper edges of a garden. From the manicured cuts of the bushes, tall and arched over like weeping willows, the ground seemed like the opposite. Vita crouched down, brushing with her hand to reveal the last of an abandoned train track. Rust iron met tobacco dirt.

When an arctic tern whipped past she looked up. There was a sign post: *Måsviken*[1].

Fruit resembling purplish stones hung in and out of the bushes. Like out of a gymnast's floor routine, Vita strutted into the garden, plums dropping, red squirrels trailing behind her.

"Hurry up," she said, looking at the man behind her.

Vita was abroad, alone, as independent as she wanted to be. She was, not as the restaurant had seen her — a disposable worker, a server's assistant — but the leader she had envisioned. She was improvising, dancing quickly from magistrate to vanguard.

---

1 – gull cove (Swedish)

XXI
a social or romantic appointment or engagement

Vita wandered with the man into *Viollunden*[1] and sat on a tree stump. There was porch sunlight. Damp songbirds hummed.

She was with someone who knew this trail much better than her.

"This is where I pick wild blueberries," he said. He pointed towards a low bush. She had been walking for half an hour into a place she had never dreamt of.

"You forage," she said.

"N..not exactly," he said. "In the summers this is where my family used to walk."

"That's nice," she said. Summer for her would happen after the harvest season. In autumns she used to dry grapes so they would become more concentrated. It was a specialty of her village which required her work from seven a.m. to eight p.m. The sun would beat, and insects bite. All relatives — uncles, aunts, her nieces — as a family they would pick the grapes, cutting leaves away from the vines, trudging buckets into large bins, spreading grapes across the backyard before fermentation.

"And you?" he asked.

"The park," she said. The park next to her house. It was not a vacation.

---

1 – violet grove (Swedish)

XXI

"Ah," he said. The sunlight faded from his face. She decided a while ago they would sit awkwardly on the same stump.

"We… we can keep going if you like," he said.

Vita had walked from her house, a house in a village with more dirt roads than trees, to a bus stop, forty-five minutes away. She had taken the bumpy bus ride to a bigger village, and from there walked twenty minutes to school.

"No, let's pick blueberries," she said.

XXII
danger

Vita continued her holiday in Stockholm. She stepped off the train platform.

This is nice, she thought.

She knew little of its people, government, agriculture, or means of livelihood, but she knew it was nice in the summer. It was not too hot.

She wanted to swim. She had heard the city had many quiet lakes and subdued attention. This was perfect, though. She hated big beaches, the show-it-alls of a summer reign.

She took a train to one of the quieter islands in the city. She wandered down a path, bringing with her a backpack and a canteen of water. She wore a bathing suit under her dress.

Her sandals pattered until they smacked the final edges of a path. She saw the lake emerge in front of her.

She also saw a pack of dogs, with the owner nearby. From afar they looked cute, and she decided to edge a little closer to them. As soon as she put her right hand out the dogs' long tongues turned to a box of sharp teeth. They raced towards her, barking, deafening the landscape. The owner wasn't paying attention, but quickly turned to see Vita in a haze of fear.

"Hey!" the owner shouted.

The dogs retreated and Vita tried to say sorry over and over and

XXII

the owner was shouting but she was about to cry and stopped. She kept going.

She got to a bench at the high point of the lake. She saw no one around her, and placed her backpack down. She kicked off her sandals, feeling her feet sink into soft ground, and feeling the blisters on her hands. There was no hot plate to burn her fingers.

She stepped towards the lake. Her feet were in the earth. She admired this moment, and breathed in. Quickly though she had taken another step and lost her balance, tumbling clumsily towards the lake, trying to stop her momentum but couldn't, each footstep jagged, dirt kicking way up as she had to let herself fall into the water.

The water was shark cold, at least to her. She looked around to see if anyone was watching, and no, she was alone, she was okay. It was freezing but the sun was shining and no one would laugh at her.

It was her first opportunity to see the lake from within. She saw docks that rooted its edges, as well as houses that grazed just past them. She shifted her eyes to a hill near the dock. There was a spot of color, just like her bathing suit, but it was stronger. Titanium yellow struck against lake soil. It was a man on a bench, reading.

She stared a bit too long, and he looked up from his book. He saw her, but had lowered his head to write something down.

She felt the cold water and forgot that moment, continuing her swim. After a while the whip of her strokes couldn't be distinguished from the birds skirting across the water. People jumped into the lake, and it didn't bother her, but she had enough courage for the day.

She swam to a large rock at the edge of the lake, near her bench, and pulled herself up. She sat dripping.

XXIII
a preliminary part, as of a book, musical composition, or the like, leading up to the main part

Scribbled along the margins were questions. Where they were going, why they were going now.

Joel looked up to see the lake. Clouds, docks, and houses rippled.

Where did they find the courage?

When he put on his bathing suit this morning he thought it was courage enough. It felt like tight raincoat wax against his legs.

He tried to simplify his questions. He attempted to remember all the places he had gone that day. The museum, the park, a new island. No, first the city center and then a new island. Remembering it in order wasn't the priority.

This afternoon he would focus on color. He was at a Swedish lake thus he would see a bluish sunset. Earlier this morning, he had noticed the city had very few benches.

According to the novel he was reading, a book about emigrants, generations of families would settle in peace. He crossed out one question and added another. He wondered which families would be remembered.

He saw something in the periphery, a young woman swimming. He couldn't tell if she was someone who frequented the lake. He wasn't adept with faces, or anything visual. His expertise was flowers, and how they smelled, thinking people could discriminate in the same way.

XXIV
sjö, insjö[1]

"Would you like a towel?" he said.

Vita looked up at Joel. His hand was outstretched, as if presenting an entrée.

"You can borrow it," he said.

Fifteen minutes ago she had seen him as faraway yellow titanium. Close up he was tall, and his eyes were the same deep blue color of the lake.

"Thank you," she said. She grabbed the towel from him, and wrapped it around her body. She was still dripping.

"Sure," he said. "Just return it to me later." He walked off.

"What do you mean later?" she said.

He turned and crouched down to open his backpack, searching for the book he had been reading. He ripped out a sheet and scribbled something on it.

"I live here," he said, providing his address. "Just stop by tomorrow."

"Okay," she said, her feet still dug into the ground.

He walked towards a small path that led up to a main road.

---

1 – lake (Swedish)

XXIV

He turned around briefly, looking right at Vita.

"Fourth story!" he shouted. "Macal!"

She held the torn page of the book in her hands. It was page xxi. INTRODUCTION, in small caps.

XXV
a formal presentation of one person to another, in which each is told the other's name

INTRODUCTION

Dalvägen[1] (it's more like a meadow)
Where did they find the courage?

fourth story. Macal.
log, I was bench, at the lake. path towards main road
yellow trunks

larkspur, snapdragon, hyacinth, rosemallows, foxgloves

---
1 – valley road (Swedish)

XXVI
the slightest mistimings

Vita wandered to a nearby park. She sat on a swing.

In a kitchen not far away, water was boiling. Vita couldn't hear the kettle humming. She thought she had heard the birds.

Moments earlier Joel had walked out to his garden. He had gone to clip lemon balm, but saw yellow flowers in the distance. He walked to them. There he had changed his mind, and picked *johannesört*[1] for his tea. Beyond him Vita was swinging. Just a few steps more and he could've seen her.

Vita was swinging as his tea was steeping. She was thinking of her day at the lake, and the man she had met.

While the tea was cooling, the man laid out his clothes for the night. He'd wear pyjamas that his nephew had picked out. They were palm-tree patterned. He wanted to go to California.

In the last minute of sunset Vita stopped the swing. She addressed a postcard home.

"The vacation I needed," she wrote.

Vita quickly stashed the postcard in her backpack. She wanted to make the train before darkness. As she hurried away, midges moved in and danced around the swing.

---

1 – St John's wort (Swedish)

XXVI

Pyjamas on, Joel stepped towards the kitchen window and admired what he had seen that evening. One of the many things in the fading light he could not see was that the flowers in his mug were blooming.

XXVII
the process of concentrating on and becoming expert in a particular subject or skill

Vita peered at the front of the apartment building. It was gray. The paleness of it met the sky in peace.

She opened the front door and walked up the three flights of stairs to the fourth story. She turned to see a row of wood doors with the name MACAL written on one of them. She stepped towards the door and knocked.

"Yes?" a man answered. She couldn't recognise the voice.

"It's me," she said. "The girl… the woman."

There was no answer.

She tried again.

"I could use another introduction," she said.

Joel opened the door. "From the loch," he said.

She didn't respond.

"I sound so pretentious when I say that, don't I," he said.

"Yes," she said.

"Meet me downstairs," he said. He closed the door.

Vita waited outside. She could hear him trot down the stairs, finally moving through the front entrance. He was carrying a sheet of paper.

XXVII

"A new introduction," he said.

She looked down. It was a copy of INTRODUCTION.

They stood in silence for a brief moment. She tried not to look at him. She thought of the lake, bringing it to her in his eyes. It made looking at him easier, but at the same time impossible. The lake was beautiful.

"Shall we go for a walk?" he asked.

XXVIII
categorisations

When Joel told her he used to sell perfume, it didn't strike her as the most direct route to becoming a doctor.

"How could it possibly help you?" she asked.

"It could, possibly," he said.

"How," she pressed.

The path they were walking on had flowers.

"What flower is that?" he asked.

"What?" she said.

"E120," he said.

"E…," she said.

"I categorize each smell," he said. "A–Y. Each letter represents a family. E's mostly flowers."

"Sounds like a bad system," she said.

"I'm sorry, what?" he said.

"You arbitrarily design something with letters of the alphabet, on top of another system of numbers, with, wait! A–Y, not even A–Z."

"Each compound has a top, middle and base note," he said.

"Are you defending your system?" she said.

XXVIII

"0 would mean the top note doesn't linger at all," he said. "It would mean you're smelling the middle note."

"I don't think I'd want you as my doctor," she said.

"I'm not into role-play," he said.

"I'm sorry, may I speak to the manager?" she asked.

"My practice wouldn't have a manager," he said. "This isn't some tourist's bar."

Vita pulled on her dress, smoothing it out.

"Doctor, I'm so so sorry for bothering you at this late hour," she said. "But there was a customer who ordered a K302 and I didn't know what to do when he fainted but as you know, you're the only one who might understand what he's saying, and well, I brought him here and —

"Please, Miss Vita," he said.

"Just call me Vita, doctor," she said.

"Joel," he said, extending his hand.

"I'm sorry… Joel. I know your patient is not breathing, but —

"Don't worry about him. He's not the only concern," he said.

"Yes, you're right. Well, you see, doct- Joel. You haven't answered my initial question. And you still haven't told me what type of flower that was."

The flower was now in the distance. They had stumbled upon a park.

"How should I know?" he said.

Vita lowered her head and looked away.

"I333" he said.

"I?" she said. "But you said E's mostly flowers…"

"Well," he said, pausing to fix his posture. "If we're being technical, your initial question was at the lake. 'What do you mean by later?' and ehm…" he stumbled, pausing again. "I meant later

XXVIII

because I wanted to see you, I333."

Vita said nothing.

"No, really…" he said, blushing. "You're the most irreverent person I've ever met, and well, no one usually argues with me like that…about perfume… It feels slightly insane, asking someone out when we're —

"*Oh, dottore, fermati mentre sei in tes*[1]—"

"It's *johannesört*," he said, interrupting. "I heard doctor… I… well, I make tea with it."

---

1 – ih doctor, stop while you're ahe— (Italian)

XXIX
a juxtaposition of rational and irrational imagery

After a couple of weeks and a different island for each date, Vita and the doctor thought to take a long weekend together. They decided on Gotland.

On the ferry, Joel saw Vita leaning against the window.

"Vita," Joel said.

Vita didn't reply.

"Boston awaits me," Joel continued.

Vita was drifting off. To their right was sunny water. She had arrived to Castiglione della Pescaia, but barely.

She and her friend Maria had darted from the restaurant, passing suits and tourists, twisting their luggage through the cobblestones.

They had twenty minutes to get from Monti to Termini.

Their train was at 13:57. They got there at 13:53, looking at the timetable, not finding Grosseto, the closest a train would take them.

Vita approached a train attendant.

"Excuse me, but I'm looking for Grosseto," she said.

"On the timetable," he said, pointing.

"No," she said. "Look," pointing at her ticket. It wasn't there.

"No," he said, pointing at 16:24 on her ticket. "You leave then."

XXIX

She knew this was wrong and her friend searched elsewhere.

"Platform 17!" she shouted.

They rushed on the train and sunk into their chairs.

As the train started, moving past the iron tracks into hay and horses, stripping against the coastline, sea at last, their eyes slowly weakened.

"Ever wish a visit?" he said.

The thought of it was so heavy that it was better to speak in half demands, and then see. The water had taken most of his vision.

"It's beautiful," she said.

Joel thought of the brownstones. "It's Roman brick" he said, making Vita feel like she was destined to like something similar. "Just younger."

XXX
situated somewhere between categories

Now that Vita was back from vacation, Zufo became more confident. Vita was hurrying around the kitchen. He too began hurrying around.

"Vita!" he chirped.

Before he could get in another word she was off. He scribbled on the menu chalkboard "coffee?", noticing she was writing so much now, thinking he could also get her attention this way.

Vita was slouched against the floor in the back. Lines were swirling. She was writing a letter.

XXXI
the etymological connection is probably due to the resemblance to
a grenade or old-fashioned bomb and may today possibly also be
regarded as a reference to the very high calorie density of the recipe

Zufo was baking *bomboloni*. This had been his best batch, puffy and stuffed with warm pastry cream. He had scrapped this recipe twice, once when his old boss Axel had him reprimanded,

"cold cream!" "*pas frais*[1]!" Axel shouted.

the other when Vita had stolen the dough.

"Where is it?" Zufo snapped. He was in the back of the pantry looking for the doughnuts he was proofing. He found Vita and a carton of *gelato*[2].

"What is this?" Zufo asked.

Vita looked at him and shrugged.

"There were leftovers," she grinned.

"Hooligans!" Zufo snapped. "I was making a batch!"

"I'm sorry Zufo," Vita said, licking her spoon. "Let me make it up to you," she said.

Zufo was surprised.

"You gonna watch this time?" he said.

Vita pushed the letter away from her.

---

1 – not fresh! (French)

2 – a type of ice cream (Italian)

XXXI

"Yeah, c'mon," she said.

"Okay well," he said. Zufo rolled up his sleeves.

"I would argue the recipe is easy, it's in the timing. The customer walks in at 6:00 and is exhausted, groggy, shot. You feel me?"

Vita nodded.

"No one appreciates it at 6:00. When a kid walks in, though, afternoon, say after school, what's better than a *bomboloni*, piping hot?"

Vita was looking at Zufo's eyes the entire time. She had never seen him this excited.

"The kid says 'hey mister,' ignorant of course that I got nine years of baking experience and a *stage* at *Maison Axel*."

"And I say, dusting off my hands, wiping them on my apron, you know I'm working and got that flour dust look."

Zufo's eyes were the blue that strikes cobalt against powdered brick.

"I say 'of course that'll be a thousand lira[1]'," Zufo said. "And the kid rummages through her pocket giving me coins that add up to six hundred, maybe seven, but who cares I've served this kid the finest bomboloni she'll have ever eaten."

When imitating the dusting of his hands, she noticed his forearms.

---

1 – Italy's pre-Euro currency

XXXII
collision of aims

"You know what's silly, Vita?" Zufo asked. "I didn't really know what falling in love meant."

They were walking on a path near the restaurant. It was their first of many breaks that afternoon.

"And then I met Axel," he said.

Vita seized up. She didn't like these conversations, particularly with Zufo.

"I heard him say once, '*je suis tombé amoreux*[1].' I didn't really think about, but do you hear what he's saying?" Zufo looked for a yes.

"No," Vita said.

"Tombé in love... it sounds like you're tumbling, like, like, stumbling into it. You really feel it, don't you?"

"No, Zufo," Vita said.

Zufo stepped back a little.

"What do you say in Italian, eh?" he said.

"*Mi sono innamorata*[2]," she said.

---

1 – I've fallen in love (French)
2 – I've fallen in love (Italian)

XXXII

"Doesn't sound as good, does it?" he asked.

"It sounds fine to me," she said.

"Just fine?" he prodded.

"Zufo I've *tombé*'d with someone else." Vita went quiet. She didn't look at Zufo.

XXXIII
a sprawling, cosmopolitan city with 3,000 years of narrative

Thunder struck the apartment.

Vita was startled. She checked the clock. It was midnight. She was supposed to take the bus to Termini in the morning. She was leaving, and this was awful timing.

She was at her friend's apartment. Chiara told her she would be sleeping, but just to wake her goodbye.

Vita assembled her espresso. She opened the coffee tin and breathed in. C321.

The grounds packed in metal, the click of the gas, the bubbling of ready — these were all moments to enjoy.

Two quick sips and she was off.

"*Buon giorno e ciao*[1], Chiara." Vita peeked into her friend's bedroom. Chiara looked at peace. It had been years since they had seen each other, and because of that it felt like they were little girls again. Chiara had liked to sleep in, even if it meant missing breakfast or a kiss. Vita didn't bother to wake her.

When Vita closed the giant door to the complex, she admired its *frapp*[2]. A gilded lion's mane and a ram's roar, all captured within one knock.

---

1 – hi and bye (Italian)
2 – invented word for door knocker, from the French *frapper* (Franglais)

XXXIII

She got to the bus stop and saw lines of people smoking at the curb. She stopped. It wasn't just thunder striking. The union had decided to protest.

"Shit," she muttered.

Vita gave a pained look to the man next to her. He smiled. She gripped her luggage and kept going. No type of strike would stop her.

As she was hauling it through Rome, tie shops patterned most streets. She passed ruins.

She would never travel alone again. In fact, she was in the most seductive city of them all, and here she was. Stop she said. Y333. The smell of sweat after a journey. He had said all sweat smells gross, unless you like the person.

XXXIV
the practice of growing a series of dissimilar or different types of cultures in the same area in sequenced seasons

Vita's story was mostly Vita's. Thomi was never supposed to get too involved, but the more he heard about her, the more he was curious, the more he adopted himself into the family's history. Why not, for example, get rid of the train station for something more modern? An airport.

Thomi circled back to the Venetian, the man in the Dublin airport Vita could've flirted with.

He was lying there on a couch, bearded, long green cargo pants, and soft striped socks.

He looked back a couple of times but it could've been anyone. He was cute. A couple was sitting next to him, there were no seats to arrange a conversation.

Vita got up to give up. But before she turned away, he sat next to her, needing the outlet to charge his phone. They looked at each other, him neutral and her stunned.

"Is that shaving cream?" she asked.

He took off the cap to show her. It was deodorant.

"Where are you headed?" she asked.

"Berlin," he said. "Well, Kyoto," he added.

"Ah," she said. "What's there?"

XXXIV

"I'm visiting my *amorosa*[1]," he said. Remembering this moment was a blur. The whole conversation here on could've been in Italian but him visiting his lover was the playful sting.

"So you're not German," she said, fatigued, draining her English.

Her stare was so serious, it was adorable.

"Italian," he said. "*Veneziano*[2]."

Thomi wondered if she had been born there, he would be visiting her.

"What a brutal language," he said, shaking his head.

She looked over to the gate. The Berlin sign was flashing.

"Time to catch your flight," she said.

"Yep," he said.

"*Buon viaggio*[3]," she said.

"You too," he said. "*Ciao ciao*."

She sighed.

Everyone seemed to be boarding at once: Berlin BER, Rome FCO, London LGW, Paris CDG, Lisbon.

Some people were sipping coffee. It was raining. Many lay flat down on the couches. One man in particular was wearing a nice suit. Light eyes, dark eyes, olive features and a goose down jacket.

"*Veneziano*," she said. She couldn't help but be disgusted, but Thomi didn't think of her story that way. She had briefly introduced herself to a life elsewhere.

Maybe one day she would meet him again. The chances were slim. The chances were none, actually. But she was comforted by the chance to go somewhere. She didn't know but chose to at least begin to know. What a beautiful...

---

1 – lover (Italian)

2 – Venetian (Italian)

3 – safe travels (Italian)

XXXIV

"*Ehi scusami ma ho chiesto*[1] —" someone interrupted.

Thomi wondered if Vita had been born in Venice, lakes would've taken on less meaning. The Stockholm lake in particular. She would've lived amongst canals and astral reverberations of Renaissance and Gothic palaces. Veneziano, in the end, would've meant being born with no roads.

---

[1] – excuse me but I asked (Italian)

four

2014
Alto Adige; Italy

2015
New England, California; USA

XXXV
playing with electrons

"Let me know if you get any room,"
You can't use that command right now...
You can't use that command right now...
Tanadien tells Antonica: 39 mnk lfg
Kilgerenski tells auction: WTS Shining Metallic Robes 2krono; Flowing Black Silk Sash 1krono 1k plat; Executioner's Hood 100 plat PST
Dailor tells Antonica: 40 Rogue LFG
Astral tells General2: Looking to join the most tinkerific players on the server? Wild Gnomes is now recruiting. Progression-firsts, every expansion. PST for more info!
Xeon tells auction: WTS Elixir of Greater Concentration 30pp/stack; Blood of the Wolf 35pp/stack; Potion of Unlife Awareness 40pp/stack

Anaya tells Ranger: WTS Ivy Etched Gauntlets and Tunic PST

Luca was sitting at his computer scrolling through a video game. This is how he met people. From Louisiana, California, France, Sweden — it didn't matter where because the Internet had collapsed his time zones.

He had his glass of anisette set on the desk. He preferred to play at night when he was lonely. He couldn't go out and spend money.

"Sorry all full mate," Trow said.

Trow was an enchanter from the UK. Luca wanted to play with

XXXV

him because he could charm goblins. And he had three more hours before he could go to bed and pass out in the morning.

Luca decided to watch Anaya tradeskill. He etched ivy into a small ringmail tunic, the emerald color foraged from the leaves of the elven forests.

Luca repoured himself a glass, tasting the licorice that melted free into the night's Faydark, the wood elves hiding behind ledges, lurking, smiling at Luca and curious if he could brew some for them.

"I don't know the recipe," he typed. He felt bad that he was sharing something personal to people he didn't know, well, people he hadn't met directly. He pushed his chair away from the desk. The computer was emitting light. It set against the big windows of his room, howled by the moon.

Luca stopped by the kitchen. He grabbed a block of Parmesan and forked off a crude crystal-like hunk. He tried to imitate his mother. She would crack Saltines in a glass, pouring buttermilk, easy wheat floating upwards.

XXXVI
a series of thoughts, images, and sensations occurring in a person's mind during suspended consciousness

Sometimes Stefano would appear with a large bike and a huge grin. He was the kid Luca used to take care of. Stefano challenged Luca to race him up and down the paths where streams stood. Hiding was his father, smoking, "Shh not a word!" he'd say, and onwards Stefano would go, knowing Luca was slow when darting through the trees.

"Can you say '*bonsoir*[1]'?" Stefano asked, laughing.

Luca had let Stefano take his phone, but he played along.

"Bonswah," Luca said.

"Bonswah!" Stefano chirped. As he charted fast along the stream he would pretend to swat away little flies. "Swah swah swah!"

"*Bonsoir*!" Luca shouted.

"Oh not bad!" Stefano said, "not bad" "not bad" his voice fading in the distance. He had caught up to his father.

"*Papà* can we take Luca to tennis?" Stefano said.

Luca wished he would've said yes.

---

1 – evening; good evening; hello; bye (French)

XXXVII
a large lake and a source of water

Deep in the forest Luca was out on an open sea. For twenty years it was a paradox Luca refused to believe. A poet was right again.

"You're not thinking," she said.

Asa stood along the border of the reservoir. She slid her hands through the fence, tapping her fingertips against rusted backs of the chainlink.

"Are you listening to me?" she asked. She was taller than Luca. This never bothered him, but it definitely mattered to his mother.

Luca imagined himself as a cliff giant, tall enough to stare beyond the water into the forest. The pine trees dwarfed against the horizon. Birds the size of polkadots crossed in and out of the trees.

"Hello, Luke..." Asa said.

"Yes, yes," Luca said. "I'm here."

"Uh hello?" Asa asked. "I can't tell if you want to be here."

Luca put his hands on the top of the fence.

"No, I do," he said. "I just wish more people did." He thought of his old high school friends, and his father.

XXXVIII
a place of residence; a family or family lineage

Kirk had promised Luca's mother that the divorce would be quick.

"Those sculptures are worth four hundred fucking thousand dollars," she said.

"That's a lot of fucking," Kirk said.

Elisa looked at the flowers.

"Do you have any sense of sacrifice?" she asked.

Kirk thought for a moment as he looked at Elisa. "Your mother didn't."

Elisa kept quiet. All she could think to do was open the fridge door. She grabbed a carton of eggs. She placed it on the counter as she heated a cast iron pan. The click of the gas intervened. It relaxed her.

When Elisa cracked a yolk into butter and black and it started to sizzle, she settled. Kirk was still leaning against the counter.

"Aren't you sick?" he asked.

Elisa stood with her back to Kirk. The carton was far to her right, but she didn't dare to turn her head. She moved her hand slowly against the counter until she felt an egg. She dropped it onto the floor.

"Elisa…" Kirk interrupted.

XXXVIII

She dropped another egg onto the floor. It cracked in half just like the first one. She smiled. She could not see but imagined the spots of plasma against the wood.

"Why don't we get a doughnut," he offered. "Something sweet."

One by one Elisa continued to drop eggs on the floor. The wood streaked as pine trees outside swayed in the wind. As her bare feet soaked in yolk and the pan's steam started to burn she tossed an egg behind her. Elisa's hand started to drip, and she started to laugh. Kirk never wanted a rug in the kitchen. It covered the beautiful wood, he had said.

It wouldn't be a rug passed down.

XXXIX
(especially in Italy) a shop selling pastries and cakes

I want the sugar rattle,
Selma piped shaking warped metal
sweet powder over Tomas
crouched t-shirt and little doughnuts

XL
vigor of expression

"And that's how we left it," Elisa said.

Thomi stood by the kitchen counter, looking at the wood floors. They were spotless. He wondered how many eggs she had cracked.

"Phff," Thomi said. "This is maybe why your mother is forgotten, *non*?"

Elisa looked out the window up towards the sky, clouds tinted obsidian, like bruises.

"Vita's become like the floors, clean, polished, yes, ha," Thomi said.

She remembered now. The clouds were the same color, black and puffy.

"She's not," Elisa said.

Elisa stared at the clouds and saw the storm unfurl again. She was with Vita but Vita was not there with her. It looked like her but it was the pond water ripping past the wind. It flooded the banks of grass, the white birds fluttering away, thin plant stalks bending and swaying. Beach plum petals floated down from the bushes to the deck and melted into planks.

XL

"Yes, not for you, she is never someone else, hm?" Thomi said. "Maybe you're, like *très*[1] angry, *sotrès*[2] angry, good new word, yes? *Sotrès* angry that you're not letting her be someone different."

Thomi reached into Elisa's liquor cabinet and poured himself a glass of pastis.

"You've fixed her in memory," he said, dropping an ice cube into his glass. "But you need to let her flicker."

Thomi pictured Vita within the plant stalks, a straw woman, jumping up and down, waving at Elisa. The beach plum petals appeared to deliquesce as they landed on her shoulders, Vita holographic in her presence. The air was hot, as was Elisa's burning rage, the relationship with her mother smudged between feelings and landscapes. Elisa took one stalk and wrapped it around her fingers, attempting to cut off circulation.

---

1 – very (French)
2 – an invented word meaning so very (Franglais)

XLI
**sleep lightly
briefly**

Asa was sunbathing by the reservoir. This was as it seems, bizarre, since the town pool was open and anyone she could've wanted to hang out with were there. The pool shack had even built a little café.

She hated how summer melted minds. Tank tops and jackknives were her friends' priorities, and while Asa wanted to be fit, she thought mind and body resolutions just became body. Even in a town that wasn't crowded, the reservoir was where her and Luca got away from it all.

She had dozed off with a book floating above her belly button. Luca called her a rebel because she read banned literature.

"Cleo Cleopatra you rebel of the forest," he taunted.

"Go away you twut," she said.

They invented names for each other that were nearly offensive, their mind and body exercise.

The sun skirted three o'clock. Pine needles slowly drifted onto her body, first to her legs and forearms, then forehead. She was Luca's Cleopatra.

"What're you thinking about today?" he asked.

She was half asleep, not paying close attention to which Luca was talking. It could've been him spying on her again, or she could've been imagining it. Living with their parents drove them to be in each other's heads.

XLI

"The lake," she replied.

"Oh the lake," he said. "What a novel landscape."

"How can water be considered a landscape?" she asked, instigating a debate. There was no reply.

At this point she knew she was beyond what most people could tolerate as normal. Her father might've thought she was crazy, and she'd say "No, I'm creative," but she didn't care because she trusted her imagination. She let herself be playful, what an elementary school might've permitted, within the boundaries of her mind, in which there were no true limits, so yes she did pretend that she was talking to a bird.

"Got ya, Scrapdap," Asa said.

"Scrapdap, hm, never heard that nickname before," the bird said.

Her eyes were still closed.

"Why don't you see the lake from above?" the bird asked.

"I reckon it," she said.

"Is that English?" the bird asked.

Asa opened her eyes. It was a giant bird.

"Oh my God!" she screamed.

The bird's pale yellow feathers were outshone only by deep black stare of its eyes.

The bird sighed. He was much bigger than Asa, but it didn't matter. He was hurt by the tautness of her voice.

"I want to show you something," the bird said.

"No no, that's okay!" Asa said.

The bird rose and stood up on its hind legs, inching towards Asa.

"No!" Asa shrieked.

She tried to scurry backwards but was moving too slow. She turned around and scrambled, but as she stood up to sprint the bird thwacked its feathers across Asa's head.

XLII
a journey for pleasure

Asa woke up to the sky and a flock of birds. "What is this?" she screamed. She looked down. "Is that a tambourine? Why is it red!" she shouted. She didn't expect anyone to answer her.

But instantly the Lagerlöfian-throated hummingbirds fluttered around her and called out: "Bogs and forests. Bogs and forests."

Asa began to understand that the big red tambourine she was travelling over were the flooded lands near Buzzards Bay, the southern and eastern edges of Massachusetts; and she knew why it looked so flecked and multicolored. The crimson she recognised first, they were cranberries floating upwards from the night before, eighteen inches of water flittering them upwards to the surface. The jingles around the perimeters of the bogs were the forests that stretched across the entire state. The dark green ones were the American Elms, thick, glossy, and double-toothed. The silvery bands were the underside of the Balsam Fir, the conifer with purplish-brown, cylindrical cones; and the faded yellows, these were the beginning of the Fall flourish, when the leaves fell quietly and crumpled, crackling under a little Laura's hiking boots. You could hear too, the Hannahs and the Natalies, these were the talented musicians of Brookline, their elementary school violas and voices were echoing great beauty of the future. The colonial houses around them grinned muddy brick red and chopped wood brown.

The girl could not keep from squealing when she saw how lyrical it all felt together.

XLIII
the frigid season

A hummingbird let Asa down onto the leaves and little twigs of the forest. It was a blanket-white February, the trees bulwarked, sensitive to the ripples of her feet. She gasped. Her feet were sticky.

"What is this!" she shrieked.

The trees chuckled. In previous years it had been her intruding, frolicking aimlessly through the forest without a care in the world.

"Closer," they whispered. Asa tiptoed slowly in the direction of one tree. "Our walls," they continued.

She smelled a bright candy. Watery sap trickled slightly out, and she knew at once it was maple-syrup season. The bark perfumed the snow with a cider frost, a makeshift fireplace in the woods. But before she could linger anymore, one of the trees inhaled deeply. The energy of the ground bent inwards towards the tree, warping her further and further away, screaming, shouting "Stop!" and they did at once. The tree's last breath launched her up and into the closest house's chimney, tunnelling her all the way down into the black soot of leftover wood. Before she could collect herself, a large monstrous figure approached.

"Ah look, another burnt chestnut," Luca exclaimed. He reached towards Asa and grabbed her, dangling, her little yelps mistaken for a roasted chestnut shell still sizzling. He plopped her down on a cutting board. She was dizzy, but saw a cleaver skating towards her face. Fast. She pushed another chestnut in front of her and

XLIII

hack! it split into pieces. Before Luca could notice, she hid behind a black cast iron pan and watched patiently as he reheated one of the smashed chestnuts.

XLIV
to entertain someone amidst drinks and a fixed portion of time

Asa was still hiding behind the black cast iron. Between heavy breaths she could see an elegant woman, wrapped in a long silk scarf. It was dotted with orange sunflowers. It was Luca's mother. Elisa was swirling her glass of Petite Arvine, a rare imported bottle from the Valais region of Switzerland. It brought her back to the trails that night, the night her friend Jeremy raced her up that same trail in his car. He had told her about the best fondue in the area. They sped through a series of dark roads into less signage and the howled backdrop of the forest. She was sure there was no restaurant.

"Stop kidding around," she said.

"But no!" he exclaimed. "Eet is around the corner."

And around the corner opened up a view of tall black felt mountains. A little chalet and murmurs. Twenty people and no one else in a ten mile radius.

The host plopped down a boiling cauldron of cheese.

"You want the classic," Jeremy said. With a long thin fork, he pierced a cube of bread and dipped it in Raclette. The bread sank into gurgles of cheese.

XLV
the Romance language of France, also used in parts of Belgium, Switzerland, and Canada, in several countries of northern and western Africa and the Caribbean, and elsewhere

Back in Boston, Elisa helped herself wake up in the Valais. She'd look at the window, the sky dizzied by her grogginess, turning its blue perpendicular into the dinner table, forming the shallow end of a swimming pool like she'd seen in Switzerland. She dipped her body in, floating, doing laps unhurried. Asa, excited by the prospect, snuck her way to the glass of wine. As Elisa drifted off into the window, Asa climbed up the thin stem and geronimoed her way into aromas of primrose and daphne. She too floated, swimming laps to the images of raclette.

"*Maman*," Luca puffed. He sometimes spoke to her in French, love distanced by language. Elisa turned to him, but had quickly looked down to see black soot diffusing throughout her glass. Asa was still covered from the chimney.

"Aah!" Elisa gasped. She got up and ran towards the front door, opening it fast enough to hurl the wine and Asa into the white snow outside.

XLVI
the study of the way meanings have changed throughout history, e.g. late Middle English from Old French *fantasie* **from Latin** *phantasia* **from Greek 'imagination, appearance'**

The landscape was no longer what Asa recognised. "Where is the boulevard?" she said. "Where is the corner store?" she demanded. Asa flicked off leftover soot and powder, shivering. "Oh my sweet one," a pinecone said, rolling around the snow. "This is it."

XLVII
a note in spirit

Where are you?! Do you ever
think of what happened
to Stefano? I know it's crazy,
but so many times I think of
that time he took my phone
and ran out and I caught him.
To: Asa
06/25/15 03:37 pm
Re-Send   Options

And he asked why I was
playing with him and I looked
at him stunned and said
 "because it's my job?"   '
To: Asa
06/25/15 03:39 pm
Re-Send   Options

XLVI

Then he said matter of fact
"none of the other sitters
ever played with me."
To: Asa
06/25/15 03:40 pm
Re-Send   Options

XLVIII
the abstract science of number, quantity, and space

Asa was still breathing heavily. The forestling sat hunched over, entertaining herself, rolling one of the dead leaves littered by jaybirds.

"Cheer up," the pinecone said.

The pinecone crumpled up the leaf and tossed it to the side. She was bored. Looking around, she smashed acorns, pulverising oak nuts against a nearby rock.

Asa was a little scared, but the repetitive sound was soft and dull. It was a relief from the earlier events of the day.

"What're you eyeballs lookin' at?" the pinecone asked.

Asa recoiled. She forgot she was staring. In that moment she admitted to herself she didn't really know her. But she was exhausted.

"I have a better idea," Asa suggested, offering her leg. Maple was stuck to her boot. The pinecone looked at her, stunned. She hesitated, deciding whether to trust her. She would, a little. She grabbed for a long branch and scraped away some sap. It was like honeysuckle.

The pinecone had forgotten she was a stranger. "Fancy a party hat?" she asked, offering Asa the cap of the acorn.

XLVIII

The pinecone rubbed leftover sap against one of her ridges. It was the first time Asa noticed her body. There were little cuts that looked new, and what — she couldn't really tell.

She lounged against a bank of snow, her ridges billowing out. They were scars.

XLIX
an Indic language of West Boston

Elisa was rinsing her glass, the soot trickling out. The water from the tap was reflecting off the windows, the swimming pool still bottled within the sink.

"What if I make fondue tonight?" she said.

"Eh?" Luca asked.

"We have leftover bread, right?" she said. Elisa darted towards the fridge.

"It's in the basket," Luca shouted, his voice blocked by the fridge door. With her squirrel-like scamper he knew her mind was pleasantly in several places.

"Right, right," she said, pacing towards the bread basket.

She took a small loaf in her hands, and with a snap of her wrists she was *anadajing*[1] through several recipes: day-old bread fried in butter and cardamom; day-old bread soaked in water, squeezed out then dressed with lemon and olive oil; day-old bread cubed as croutons.

"No one's ever made an hour-old bread recipe," Elisa stated. Luca was holding a chestnut and half glass of easy red.

"I'm sure someone has, just never bothered to im—

---

1 – creative interpretation of *andaj*, the Bengali word 'to estimate'

XLIX

"improvise!" Elisa exclaimed.

"Eh?" Luca asked.

"Her father wasn't a licensed cook —

"Yes, we know of your first Michelin star," Luca said, nodding, peeling a chestnut, the steam fragranting.

"No, no, Jhumpa Lahiri's father. He had to use a microwave to cook *pulao*[2]. For almost a hundred people." Elisa was orating. "We're like her father… stuck without the right tools."

"We're just like her father," Luca said.

"Carbon copies," Elisa said. "As global local i.e. 'glocal' chefs, we can't ever truly copy the fondue of the mountains," she continued, thinking she was clever to repeat the word 'copy.'

"but what if we tried to make it ourselves," Luca said, muttering,

"but what if we tried to make it ourselves!" Elisa said.

---

[2] – a dish of rice, or pilaf (Persian, Hindi, Bangla from Sanskrit)

L
dipped into melting

Deep into the pan it started to swirl, dissolving downwards as heat ribboned cheese into fondue.

"Just like in the mountains," Elisa said. She took a sip of wine, and looked briefly downwards, her apron fixed against her body with spatters of previous experiments like lingonberry fritters and pink rice porridge.

"Do you think they'll show the tennis today?" Luca asked. He was flipping through channels on the TV, when he stopped. The Santa Rosa and San Jacinto mountain ranges in California were the backdrop of the Indian Wells tournament, bullet strokes contrasted with dances more eternal.

Elisa's favourite player was Jana. She floated. Elisa always saw herself moving, blurring into the court to the point where she was also the sun and dry air. More than her athleticism, though, she admired the way Jana walked to the net. It took something to smile in loss.

As daylight turned to quiet frost, the window frames darkened. Luca's body pulled closer to the television. It was something about the Boston winter flashing against a bright California sun that became ritualised within him.

Elisa stood with her glass of wine, looking at Luca. She then turned to the forest, which was trapped between the last moments of twilight. She thought that the scent of pine was different, perhaps better, trees humming one more verse as they expected darkness.

She could still see the stones. They bordered the edge of her house, and surrounding houses. Her town was one of the very few that kept the modern roads colonial. Some people hated these stones.

"*Maman*," Luca said.

Elisa had stopped paying attention. She looked down again at the pot, bubbling. The fondue was ready.

LI
in relation

"What's it like out here?" Asa asked.

They walked along the forest until they hit a big wooden ramp. Asa knew nothing of this area, she just knew it wasn't what her house looked like. The trees had black leaves.

"What're you sputtering?" the pinecone asked.

"Where are we again?" Asa asked. Her nose was bleeding.

"The everforest," the pinecone said. "Purgatory!"

Asa didn't understand what she was talking about, but it was dinnertime, and she was starving.

That evening the pinecone cooked. She had wrapped a little fish from the stream in maple leaves, and smoked it over slow heat.

"This is delicious," Asa said.

"No," the pinecone said, pausing. "But don't think you've ever picked at rancid mackerel."

Asa stopped mid-bite. She had read about emigrants who had smelled the odor of fish and tar. She was traveling to a place that was beyond the limit of her senses. She hadn't smelled such a sour. She had heard of this peculiar type of struggle, and didn't know if she should be fortunate. She decided not to make trauma, but she would listen to it. Was it the same thing?

LI

The fact that the pinecone was this aware surprised her. From the novel, she knew of the porridge hunger that killed a little girl younger than herself. She looked down at the soup spoon the pinecone had set, and trembled.

LII
with scales that open

"It's lentil soup," the pinecone said.

Asa looked at her and was skeptical.

"With some *brännvin*[1]," she added, rolling her tongue upwards. She poured a little into the pot, before opening the lid to a jar of sour cabbage.

"Stinks," Asa said.

"Try before commentary, darling," the pinecone said, ladling some soup and shreds into Asa's bowl.

She took a sip. It was pungent. "It's the good cabbage," the pinecone said. "Polish," she said, nodding.

---

1 – the Swedish term for liquor distilled from potatoes, grain, or (formerly) wood cellulose

five

1959
2002
2015
New England; USA

LIII
to adapt to the prevailing levels of senses

Luca started his run up the driveway.

Sunlight streaked the concrete. He ran into the yellow gloss, but it was brief, his last step of sun shadow. Pine trees darkened the sidewalk. He couldn't see much, but he smelt the honeysuckle. It was bright. But his next step turned into salt. It felt like he was tasting limestone, oyster shells and the fish market just up ahead.

"Lookin' for something are ya?" the fisherwoman said.

"A net of steamers, please," Luca said.

"A net?" the fisherwoman asked.

"They're in a net, right?" "A red net," he said.

"It's fixed by weight," the fisherwoman said. She then turned to the kitchen. "A pound and a half for this blonde caramel!" she shouted.

He sat at the wooden crates outside, where he dunked the steamers in broth. He looked out. He saw the sea again. The path should've had houses, but all he felt was an open dock. There were no boats. No fishermen. No mailboxes got in his way. The birds were in and out of the branches. When he hugged the path it felt like the trees got closer. He swayed the other way, towards where cars should've been, but he rocked back to the humming of the heat and the leaf gasps, he thought of himself as a hill giant, roaming with huge footsteps to and from the forest and the market by the quai where his grandmother's story was entangled.

LIV
olive oil

Luca's aunt was visiting from Italy. He remembered this day because of the fennel fronds they were chopping.

"Save them!" his mother said. She had never used that voice with him, neither chastising nor yelling — it was a yip of excitement.

His mother was slicing the onions.

"Not onions," she reminded him. "Fennel."

He didn't understand the difference because no one had ever made this salad she kept talking about. It was his aunt's recipe, something she prepared when she was visiting, why only visiting, he never understood.

There was a light tap on the door.

"It's Lucia Santa!" His mother had hurried towards the door.

"*Ciao! Ciao!*" you could hear as the embers rekindled in the fireplace. It was a bitter late April.

Lucia Santa climbed her way slowly up the stairs as he helped to take her jacket. It was heavy, made of fur. He dunked his face in it.

"*And come stai*[1], Luca?" she said, gently grabbing his face. "How are a you?"

---

1 – and how are you (Italian-American)

LIV

Lucia Santa quickly moved on to the next task and placed down a crimson jug, labeled "*D.O.O.G. Mia.*"

It was a special olive oil. Luca had heard about it before, but didn't understand the fuss. He had bought with his mother what he saw in the supermarket, the bottle with the farmer on the front and the big OIL on the back.

"Did your already prepare the fennel?" she asked his mother.

Luca saw the hill of fronds on the kitchen table and pointed. It was fragrant, it was bright, and it was the best licorice one could harvest.

"Yes it's there," Elisa said. "But I'm preparing it with pomegranates."

"You what?!" Lucia Santa snapped. "Its fennel and orange!"

"We don't have any oranges!" Elisa said.

"So you buy oranges," Lucia Santa said. "I drive with Luca, you can —

"No," Elisa said. "Those tasteless ethylene-ripened fruits?"

Luca didn't understand what was being said but he could hear his mother getting louder, her voice straining.

"Oh how could they do that," Lucia Santa. "I don't believe you, an orange is an orange."

"Industrial. Agriculture. USA," Elisa said, waving her arms around with faux Italian gestures.

"Ok we make it with pomegranate," Lucia Santa said. "But we use the good olive oil still."

Lucia Santa looked at the fennel. She knew that pomegranate seeds were much smaller than the orange segments she intended. She grabbed a large knife and started to thinly slice each fennel round like a sashimi chef would a piece of fish.

"So it's texture makes more sense when you eat it," she said, turning her head towards Luca, her one boy cooking show. He was watching every motion, quiet, observing.

LIV

Elisa arranged the fennel on a large plate that was lacquered bright yellow. The slices melted into the plate, glinting translucent.

Lucia Santa uncorked the crimson jug. She poured in cascading fashion two glugs of green gold. The fennel sunk deeper. She then cracked some sea salt and tasted it.

"Try this, Luca,"

He dipped his fingers into the shallow volume of olive oil, now magenta gold. It tasted like luxury.

Lucia Santa stepped outside onto the small deck. She breathed in the pine trees and sighed deeply.

Elisa was still at the kitchen table when Luca tiptoed over to her. He held the large lacquered plate over his head.

"*Maman*, try this!" he said.

"No thank you," she said. She was gazing at Lucia Santa on the deck, thinking of the time she dared her to eat the orange rind.

"Just one bite!" he pleaded.

"No!" she shouted. Her eyes looked like her seven year old self, pigtailed with glee and a delicate confidence.

Luca thought back to of all this as he looked at the blackened chestnuts.

"Oh Luca, are you crying?" Lucia Santa asked. She had left the door to the deck ajar, and he had wandered to find comfort.

"No," he said. He dried until he colored his face magenta gold and all he smelled was the licorice of fennel fronds. "It's just a little olive oil."

LV
in motion

"You hang those there?" Joel said.

He was looking at Vita's swimsuit. It was drying on the balcony.

"Your point?" Vita said.

"What a nonsense," he said.

"No one here tends their clothes…" she said.

"No one here in Boston dries them that way," he said.

"I'm sorry, what way?" she said.

"With strings and pin clips," he said.

Vita rolled her eyes.

"No one in Italy studies medicine in a snowstorm and when the sunlight hits, thinking 'finally vitamin D' —

"No no, it's produced endogenously from —

"Finally a drop of a beautiful day," she corrected.

"The Swedes would argue, like Bostonians, that the ray is a form of —

"Absolutely not," Vita said.

"Absolutely how then?" he said.

"They appreciate the light," she said.

LV

"No," he said.

"I swear," she said.

"You swear you heard me say what pale light," he said.

"Yes, my point," she said. "Your culture don't understand creativity."

Joel paused, and looked at Vita.

"Can't you just like my apartment?" he asked.

"If we take painting classes together, yes," she said.

"Fine," he said.

"Watercolor," she said.

"Yeah, watercolor, whichever..." he said.

It was in that moment Vita realised Joel didn't know the difference between oil and watercolor, and the reason she became interested in the two. Joel probably didn't know who John Singer Sargent was, what he painted, or what he meant to her. Sargent had studied Venice and she Boston. He too was an expatriate, or at least that was what she was beginning to think of herself. Sargent, however, was remembered. It was easy for him, drawings left all over to be preserved, archived, perhaps forged. There was no guarantee not even her family — any family — would educe the value of her story. Vita was like many people in that she was vaulted away by others before she got the chance to represent herself.

LVI
italian

Elisa was looking at a photo. Her fifth grade teacher had framed it for her over forty years ago. There was a little boy in the photo grinning, clutching a red kickball tight against his chest. It was her childhood friend Dante.

Before the teacher had taken the photo, Dante had taken the kickball from Elisa. Seconds later he darted off to some monkey bar balance beam challenge, red orb in hand.

She looked back at his face in the frame. She knew that grin would earn him, in his cowboyish words, "loot, but the good kin', fortune's mine."

Elisa remembered he had always ordered an espresso from the vending machine at school, two sugars.

"Don't worry I got this," he said, jamming two pennies to make the machine feel like it was a quarter.

"You'll get us in trouble!" Elisa said, looking around the hallway for one of the teachers.

"Nah, Elisa," Dante said, bellowing out his chest a little. "It takes thirteen seconds for the little purple plastic cup to drop down into the slot. The coffee splits in three, and before *Signora* finishes her petit dedge *voilà* it's ours." He pressed the double sugar button, crystals sprinkling out over the coffee foam.

"You want one *Signora*?" he winked, jokingly.

LVI

Elisa sipped coffee from her little cup. She had hesitated but couldn't resist smiling. It reminded her what her mother had said about him, buried once in snow with Tranströmer's poetry.

"That Dante's *en rödbrun fyrkant stark som en buljongtärning*[1]," Vita said, praising her own Swedish.

Elisa was looking at the houses outside. Even though some were a faded brick brown she thought that the little boy through both frames was collecting pine cones, blurring amongst one of the houses. There he was, a reddish square quite cute like a bouillon cube.

---

1 – a reddish square intense as a bouillon cube (Swedish)

six

*2015
New England; USA*

LVII
indulging in recollection and recreation

These summer strawberries. I'm sorry doctor:
the icebox dug into the shore. sweet cold plums.
    On bzzating farms, the race of kids
galloping exclamation marks toothless.

Vita returns to the same places.
Faint sunlight of the lakes, the train whirring
    her eyes closed while
the icebox is melting with new memories.

LVIII
a particular form or stage of civilisation, as that of a certain nation or period

Asa was a girl in flight, seeing herself more and more like a bird, on the periphery, a European café goer on rooftops and traffic lights responsible for fledgling powers of observation. She didn't drive into Boston. No, she flew into the city. She birdwatched.

A woman's husband in the Seaport district was trying to park. She saw a gentleman maybe leaving. He had a NYONGO license plate.

"*Misawa*[1]," the woman said.

The gentleman scrunched his eyebrows.

"Are you leaving?" the woman asked.

"No, no," the gentleman said.

The woman and her husband drove off, continuing to look for parking.

"Why did you say that to him?" the husband snapped.

"I was trying to help you park!" she said.

"You're white," he said.

"Oops," the woman said. "Yeah… what if he was Luhya[2]?"

---
1 – hello (Dholuo, or Luo)
2 – a Bantu group in Kenya

LIX
rebeginning

Asa began to worry there were too many worlds.

Luca was looking at the computer screen. Asa was too, but off the window's reflection. In daylight it was like the sun was buzzing, bent. She would look up at the sky, and think it was bright. She would then look at the computer screen, and think it was also bright.

She couldn't place the source of light.

The branches swayed up and down, Luca typed on his keyboard.

A halfling skirted across a cavern. His name was Fuddwin.

"Did you light the torch?" Fuddwin said.

"Yes, I stood right where the skeleton was standing," Luca said.

"Let me see," Fuddwin said.

"Right here," Luca said.

"You weren't right there!" Asa shouted.

"No, not there," Fuddwin said.

"Well where should he be?" Asa asked.

"Spam the macro," Fuddwin said.

A gray squirrel darted across the trees outside.

LIX

"Again," Fuddwin said.

"This quest is terrible," Luca said.

Acorns dropped like darts as the squirrel shook the branches.

Asa threw one at the window.

Luca stood up from his chair.

"What the," Luca said.

"Spam the macro, quick," Fuddwin said.

"I am, there's a damn squirrel that —

"This is it," Fuddwin said.

"I failed it," Luca said.

"No, no, spam it again," Fuddwin said.

Luca says, "Never say it, No Sun!"
Luca says, "The game restarts"
Luca says, "the fun has run!"

LX
the art of communication that is remarkably French: expressive, that is, not to be taken literally, charging words with dance and flirtation

Dear Stefano,

Under the advice of myself, I'm writing to you.

Do you miss me? I like to believe that you're only laughing because I say things more bluntly, without the direction of your undersecretary... I mean sister.

Américain Touch Department

oh, p.s. Thomi has the creative air… he's building the forest bar. Finally. How long do you think it'll take…?

LXI
soft and tremulous

"Luca!" Asa shouted.

Luca could barely hear who was talking.

"Luca, Luca!" she repeated, shaking his arm.

"Eh?" Luca said.

He slowly opened his eyes, dirt covering his shirt, grabbing his right leg. There was a large bruise.

"You tripped," Asa said.

"No, I was running..." Luca said.

"This stone here," Asa pointed.

Luca, still on his back, turned his neck to see the stone.

"No, I was on the path," he said.

"Yeah Cleo saw you running," Asa said.

"You saw me?" he asked.

"Come on," she said, and for the first time smacked his cheek. "Get up."

The forest looked different this time. Light was shimmering where it shouldn't.

"Luca!" Asa said.

LXII
a written, typed, or printed communication, especially one sent in an envelope by mail or messenger

Caro[1] Stefano,

How is Los Angeles? Do you miss the good coffee with me? Oh, Elisa's asking if you've used your espresso machine yet.

Luca

---

1 – dear (Italian)

LXIII
caused by high temperature

"We're near the house?" Luca asked.

"Yeah," Asa said. "Right over there."

All Luca could see were the pine trees.

"What time is it?" he asked.

Asa looked up at the branches, and last remaining sunlight, coruscating between two moss trunks.

"Six," she said.

"Eh?" he said. "I'm gonna be late for the raids," he said.

"Nah I saw Astral," she said.

"You what?" he asked.

"He's cool with it," she said. "You'll be like five minutes late."

LXIV
like a gate, or other entrance, particularly elaborate

Boog tells the guild, "Need to knock out 100 AAs"
Bug tells the guild, "01"
Baru tells the guild, "I'll bring the clr dps"

Boog, Bug, and Baru were off to experience. They buffed in the Guild Hall, a 200 sq foot area where they could gather. Baru casted Tenacity, and Aura of Devotion, spells to protect them. They were ready.

Bug set the portal to Goru`kar Mesa. He liked to talk to the vendor, a fellow gnome.

"01 0 0 10?" Bug asked. He spoke at times in binary.

"No, Bug... it's awful!" the vendor replied. Zeflmin Werlikanin was not in the mood to talk ore imports.

"But the new seals we're making!" Bug said.

"We could do without the titanium!" Zeflmin snarled.

"One Mesa sandstone, please," Boog interrupted. Sometimes Bug was blind to time, his little pink boots a telltale. He could heal for eternity, or he could talk for such; it was Boog's job to make sure he kept going. Zeflmin offered Boog the stone. For the older gnome it was a harbinger of something that would repeat itself.

"How lucky there's quartz in some of your hearts," Zeflin recited.

LXV
a dense mass of vertical or tangled objects

The trees smiled as Luca and Asa were walking through the forest.

They were trudging along, him hobbling behind her.

From afar they could've seen the deck. If they had looked up, and to their far right. It was newly shellacked. Thomi had painted it, but had kept it pale.

"That's not finished," Luca said.

"But *non*, yes it is," Thomi said. "Look."

Thomi held a Czech pilsner up to the deck's edge.

LXVI
a look past a location

The shifting color of the pilsner took Thomi back to Bordeaux, his city of subtlety between water and light.

Further inland, in the countryside, the fragile skins of grapes began to rot. Humidity damaged them.

In the same fog five kilometres away a train bulleted past, whirling into the carved out forest.

If he hadn't lived there, he would've missed this Vermeer, the top hills, the fossilized oysters below, the vineyards with urban workers, smashed together from the conditions of the morning.

Thomi considered all of this as he poured himself a glass of Sainte-Croix-du-Mont. The glass itself glinted in many directions. He pictured the different light on the faces of the cup fragmenting a collection of his memories, as if ten little pages of his life were tacked on like a storyboard exposed for the world to see, depending on which face one looked at.

LXVII
moving while thinking

While Thomi waited for the bus to arrive, he saw it pedal slowly into the station, the passengers affronted with chainlink fences, gridding nature.

He ignored the fences' metal rings. Instead he focused on the mid-morning light, vines hanging with night sky flowers.

Meters later, football fields appeared, blank green.

Voices chattered, caffeinated, long windows were flickering the light from warehouses, shrubs, and butterflies.

LXVIII
chateau ruins along the modern bus route

Thomi stepped onto the bus and sat in the middle, facing against the direction they were all going. No one cared for him as a compass.

It sped up a timeline back into former histories, chateau ruins, bricks laying in the grass, tightly squeezing through the village streets, like a city alley, Cadillac walls, cobblestones, corn stalks, the busy vineyards, rows of vines set against the dampening sun, in the shadows of twilight in tree canopies for 50 meters then back to faded light.

He arrived at Place Stalingrad central bus station. He saw an advertisement for Nestlé dairy products decorated by a Vermeer painting. Though the ad was, by someone else's definition, creative, he pitied the slick reproduction of the imagination, the warped sense of realism by a conglomerate. Industrial milk's fine art.

LXIX
not just sounds, but others

When Thomi started up his run he had split himself again between countries. He saw dried wheat fields and stone panels. He turned away from the house and ran into a blast of cookies and cream. He thought that he was developing a sense of where he was that was more personal.

He continued up the steep hill, next to a bicyclist,

"Oh it's difficult," he said, spandex tightened against the slope.

"That's sure," Thomi said.

He saw sunflowers, which didn't smell like anything, but they were *gamboge*[1], a color he swore by the sound alone should've been French in origin.

He thought he was going to pass the farmer, tending a little garden — a side project — but there was no one. He continued on.

It is difficult, he thought. When he was out of breath it was nearly impossible to detect anything, but that was the experience, feeling it when one thought there was nothing left.

He chose a path, because maybe there would've been something new.

---

1 – a partially transparent deep saffron to mustard yellow pigment. from *gambogium*, the Latin word for the pigment, which derives from *Gambogia*, the Latin word for Cambodia.

LXIX

It surprised him, because it was something old. It was deep concord grapes, and rhubarb, tart, not yet pied, it was like he was sipping cherry juice, sweet and bitter after hours of tennis. It was Boston. He wanted ice cream but this would do, back and forth, back and forth.

LXX
a château defined by the senses, i.e., not by property

"If I told you a story would you believe me?," Asa said.

"Depends what kind of story," Luca said.

"Don't be like that," Asa said.

"Like what?" Luca said. "You're the one who's been acting strange."

Asa paused.

"How was your run?" Asa asked.

"Well…" Luca said.

"Where were you running to?" Asa asked, reframing her question.

"What does it matter, where?" Luca said.

"I don't understand," Asa said.

"Why do I have to be going anywhere?" Luca said.

"Because you won't meet anyone new here?" Asa said, laughing innocently.

"Like you would know," Luca said.

"I would know, actually," Asa said.

"The point is I don't have to go," Luca said.

"Not even to travel?" Asa said.

"I don't have to go all the time," Luca said. "It just complicates

LXX

things," he continued.

"But then you won't experience new people, new places — new foods!" Asa said.

"Look what it's done to all our friends," Luca said.

"They would've left anyway," Asa said.

"I'm not so sure," Luca said. He paused. He was sure.

"Well there's choice, right?" Asa asked.

"Sometimes I don't think it's a very good idea," Luca said. "Besides, I'd prefer to attach myself here. To the *sol*[1]."

"The *sol*," Asa said.

"The soil," Luca said. "It's what Thomi says, you know, the composition of minerals, oxygen, precipitation, what we experience in a location, what we learn to like if we stay long enough in one place."

"I think you're drinking too much French juice," Asa said.

"I'm not!" Luca said. "I would even argue I'm attaching myself to the light here."

"*Le soleil*[1]," Asa joked, pirouetting.

"Haven't you ever noticed how the eyes of Swedish people dilate?" Luca asked.

"What?" Asa said.

"What's so bad about sensing one place so much it lets us like other places, it lets us appreciate other ways of living, and so in the end the more emotions you'll accept, you'll circulate?"

"Circulate..." Asa said, doubting his ability to be profound.

"That you'll let go of, that you'll radiate, that you'll let be other places and a part of," Luca said.

---

1 – ground, floor, soil (French)
2 – the sun (French)

LXX

"Now you're just confusing me," Asa said. What the hell was he talking about, she thought.

"I bet you I've been to places I don't even know I've been to," Luca said.

"Uh huh," Asa said.

"Don't you think there's something beautiful about an energy at random?" Luca asked.

"And now you're blabbering," Asa said.

"No, no," Luca said. "Like all those lakes in Stockholm. That each one has its own memories, its own relationships. But a Burgundian Stockholm lake… like a Swedish lake where you can swim in many lakes in many different towns, and still call it your sense of a place."

"Call what?" Asa asked.

"Where you can call one lake the collection of your experiences, of many places," Luca said.

"Yeah, that's why people build houses," Asa said.

"Or estates," Luca said.

"You agree with me," Asa said.

"No, I'm just saying we don't have to die of boredom by being in one place," Luca said.

"Uh huh," Asa said.

"Just a few rows of vines, or laps on the eastern side of a lake, or the path with ten less lingbonberries than the other trails of the forest," Luca said.

LXXI
sulfur dioxide

A forest wind had battered the edges of the deck. It eroded the sense of summer, the sense of everything being hot.

For a moment Luca was on his run. The air was frigid, and he could appreciate that Thomi had been somewhere else.

"He's building the deck," Luca said.

But the deck was collapsing.

The door sign said "OPEN."

Thomi went in and the wine bottles were all open. There were no corks.

He jogged up the stairs, holding the railing as he did so. When he got to the structure of planks overlooking the forest, he knew his concept for a bar was changing.

Thomi grabbed the opened bottles and stacked them outside.

LXXII
language containing an excessive amount of legal jargon

Elisa was on a flight back to Boston, ready to see Thomi's progress.

She had to pee. Badly. The seatbelt sign was still on when the flight attendant stopped her.

"No, you can't go in," the flight attendant said.

Elisa tried to step in.

"No, the seatbelt sign is on," he continued.

"I would like to pee," Elisa said.

The flight attendant slammed the bathroom door open.

"You do so at your own risk," he said.

Elisa stared into the flight attendant's eyes. He stepped back a bit. These past couple of years Elisa had had a blank look, but not this time, not today, because for the first time it hit her that Thomi was opening doors, not blocking them.

LXXIII
a candy that melts like caramel

"Is that luggage yours?" the Irishman asked.

"No, no," Elisa said. "They took it away,"

"Ah," he said. "Mine too."

LXXIV
belief in reliability, or growability

Elisa and the Irishman sat next to each other. He wasn't paying attention to her, but whenever he glanced over, it was one of her good friends from years ago. He had the same blond curly hair, the same big fists. She didn't know how to explain it.

LXXV
a graphical representation of a period of time

"How long will you work there?" Elisa asked. She was back in Boston, wasting no time to demand answers.

"I don't know," Luca said.

"You don't know?" Elisa said.

"Till it's done I guess," Luca said.

"Till it's done I guess," Elisa repeated.

Elisa's head was propped against the table, gazing out.

"What happens if it goes out of business?" Elisa said.

"*Maman*," Luca said.

"Or Thomi moves back to France," Elisa said.

"Ha," Luca said.

"You think that's funny," Elisa said.

"I think it's funny you think it's funny to joke about Thomi," Luca said.

LXXVI
a representation of a period of time by the senses

There was a pale wood veranda, empty tables, and echoes of nearby players. Some people were smoking, snacking on *canelés*, caramelised crusts of rum and vanilla, custard centres. But Thomi was watching the tennis.

The courts were clay, a crushed red-orange brick that dusted up a brilliant hue as players slid across the surface. It softly powdered their clothes, and left them feeling part of all of it. Even the side fences and hoses were lightly coated.

After a rally, he turned his head to the back fence. He saw dragonflies and lavender. They swayed towards him.

One player had saved his little treat, placing it on the courtside bench as he hit. On a changeover, he had bit into it. He then had a sip of water, and now satisfied, he trotted back to the baseline.

Thomi noticed the pastry. Its wrapper had fingerprints.

LXXVII
perhaps from Old Norse *bára* 'wave'; in middle English the term was used in the general sense 'billow, wave'

"Would you like a drink?" Thomi asked.

"What?" the patron said. She was standing, looking out at the forest. She was the first of her party to arrive.

"A beer, what the soldiers drink, etc.," Thomi said.

"The soldiers?" she said.

"You know, Coca-Cola," Thomi said.

"Ah," she said. "No, no, a beer is my sticker," she said.

"I'll be right back!" Thomi said, hurrying across the deck down the stairs.

He brought back a Mascaret.

"It's good," he said. "*Bio*[1]!"

She looked at the label. "Blonde BIO Grand Cru," it said.

"It's a brewer of that area, Gironde," Thomi said. "He makes the artisanal beer."

She took a sip.

"It lasts in your mouth," he said.

"Against the current," she said.

---

1 – organic (French)

LXXVII

She specified something Thomi thought was profound. More mascarets, yes, that's what the family needs, more tidal, less bore, ha, yes, tidal bore, what a simple way to end up against the current of a storyline.

LXXVIII
waves that converge in the troposphere

Elisa looked out to see the mountains descending into forests.

The sun was too intense for her to stare directly at what was below.

"It's apple season," the Irishman interrupted.

"Uh huh," Elisa muttered.

"He's back!" he said.

"Who's back?" she said.

"Johnny Appleseed," he said, flexing his bicep.

"That's Popeye," she said.

"Oh," he said. "What's the difference?"

A flight attendant passed through with pasta, warmed with tomato and spinach.

"His spinach isn't frozen," she said, frowning. She didn't want to hear what Thomi was going to say about her.

LXXIX
if irreality was accepted as real

Vita sat alone at a table for two. She was waiting for Luca.

"As you wish," Thomi said. He had not noticed who he seated.

Vita looked around, resting her feet.

Autumn leaves brandished in the wind, pines needles trickled down like rain.

A man passed her view.

"Excuse me, sorry," Vita said.

Zufo passed through. Vita didn't see him.

When he passed back, Vita interrupted, waving her hand.

Zufo stopped. Vita looked at him, her eyes dilating.

"Vita," Zufo said.

"Hello," Vita said.

"I… I never said sorry," Zufo said.

"Sorry?" Vita asked.

"I saw you in me," Zufo said.

"Don't be silly," Vita said.

"No, I mean it," Zufo said. He inched closer to Vita. "Where've you been?"

LXXIX

Vita hesitated.

"I could've asked you that," Vita said.

"I never went anywhere," Zufo said.

"Then why are you sorry?" Vita asked, expecting a long story.

"I'm… I'm," Zufo said, his voice trembling.

Thomi was wiping down a table, eavesdropping on their conversation. He giggled knowing the play in front of him was like shadow puppetry, him propping up who said what.

"You don't have to be here," Vita said.

Thomi reset the table. He traced the length of the chairs, running his fingernails along the leather of the seats.

"Could.. coulda been us, Vita," Zufo said, his voice still quavering. "I'm… I'm, yeah I know I didn't have to make it like this, but well, you're the girl on the bus and that's the best way I could see it. No trains, no boats, no nothing — just you and me nearby. You… you took off. You traveled farther than I thought you would."

LXXX
dedicated to memories that keep forming

Dusk wine was spilling out among the leaves when Asa and Luca arrived.

The bottles hung, overlooking them.

"Why isn't it finished?" Luca demanded.

Thomi was walking around the deck, arranging chairs that his friends had built for him.

As he was repositioning a bench, he picked up and tossed needles and cones back into the forest.

Asa was there, as he was, and many others.

LXXXI
a brief respite of temperatures like this, at night

Cyclists stopped to enjoy the forest bar. They left their bikes at the entrance, yellow flags flapping in the slowing wind.

The backs of their jerseys had names like "GINIX" "VASH" "SONNYVIPER" and "CARTO." They were all guildmates from Luca's video game.

They sat at a long dining room-like table, twelve of them, a team, but more like a family. "GOOPLINK" had his jersey on backwards.

After they tasted some of the bar's delicacies, slouched from exercise, they left. It was night time.

The cool air was against Thomi's face, the lamplight dim. He tried to serve himself water but spilled in darkness. He sat alone, with Elisa.

LXXXII
in attempt to form a spoken or written account of connected events

"Did I build it?" Thomi asked

"No," Elisa said.

"*Ah bon*[1]?" Thomi retorted.

Elisa folded a napkin.

"That's not how my mother met Joel," she said.

Thomi poured Elisa a glass of anisette.

"Please inform me then," he said.

---

1 – I see; really (French)

LXXXIII
a willed apparition

Vita sat at a table in a corner, watching Thomi and Elisa. She was obscured by darkness.

"They didn't meet at the lake," Elisa said.

She sipped the licorice from her glass. Thomi did not move.

"They met because of the lake," Elisa said.

Thomi's eyes widened. He lit a cigarette.

"When two people arrive at the same thing it's not random," she said.

Thomi leaned over the deck's edge and tapped ash out into the forest.

"I don't see her traveling like that," Elisa said. "Maybe she was…" she continued. "But… but it doesn't explain why I don't feel a part of it."

LXXXIV
a long internal speech by one actor interrupted by other internal speech

"That's bullshit," Vita said.

Thomi was adjusting his sweater. Elisa had left to grab a bottle of wine from the cellar.

"Don't you see she's foolish?" Vita asked.

Thomi was remembering the bookstore. The wood blue, maybe he could've painted the doorway to the bar such a color. If he had done so earlier, maybe he would've changed his mind. He liked royal colors.

Vita felt her coat pocket and left a letter on the table.

Thomi did not think he was in this forest because of what he imagined. Elisa didn't pay him for his creativity, even though that is some of what he brought. She didn't pay him for how he built the bar either, such a new concept, a forest bar, who could say no! Why she couldn't think of it herself, he didn't fully understand, but feeling her anger, he knew some people were better suited for this type of profession. He was here because of what he imagined for others elsewhere

LXXXV
a supernatural (mis)representation

Vita never saw Luca below. He was overhearing the conversation, wondering how he belonged in all of this.

He thought if he had studied Swedish instead of Italian, he would've applied to different jobs. Not necessarily jobs in Sweden over jobs in Italy, but maybe he would've never apprenticed as a baker.

Asa said he always liked to imagine himself elsewhere. Like when he was in the vines, he thought of himself as an ice giant. He wandered the northern parts of the Earth, and as he stepped shards of his body melted into the snow.

LXXXVI
the year or place in which wine, especially wine of high quality, was produced

Down in the cellar Elisa had a moment to think about what she said to Thomi. She didn't know her mother through stories she told herself.

She took one of the bottles in her hand. It was the bottle of vintage red Thomi had kept. A viticulteur had produced a good year of grapes. 2007 was therefore a good year, at least for Thomi.

Elisa raised the bottle and smashed it against the wall.

LXXXVII
a hobbied observer

Asa remembered Elisa with the scarf. Light had shone from the windows onto her orange sunflower silk. She looked at peace in memory.

Down in the cellar she was crying. Asa was spying. It wasn't clear if Elisa had cut herself deeply, but the ruby wine in cellar darkness had made it impossible to know what was blood and what wasn't. Asa thought of the pinecone, and her scars, and thought maybe she too had smashed something.

LXXXVIII
an elaborate figuration

"Is it a mistake to imagine?" Thomi asked.

Vita and Thomi sat together, him mid-cigarette and her mid-sip of coffee.

"Your imagination saved us," Vita said.

Thomi had given up. He returned to the royal blue door frame, and the collection of books labyrinthed across the store.

"I don't regret anything I created," Thomi said. "As long as it's for the good of others."

Vita laughed, realising he needed her help.

"Do you know that fingerprint canelé you keep obsessing over?" Vita asked.

"The tennis court canelé?" Thomi said.

"Yes, the that one," Vita said. "I think they're your fingerprints."

"That's a good one, yes, ha!" Thomi said.

"I'm serious," Vita said. "You've upset everything, even the pastry wrappers. It's beautiful."

Thomi ignored what Vita was suggesting.

"Maybe I'll just keep inventing possibilities," Thomi said. "Eventually someone will meet someone, and families will start, and then communities will be important again."

LXXXVIII

Vita felt bad for Thomi. It was as if he was struggling to theorize why he and Elisa were so unhappy.

"I'm a bad bartender, you know," Thomi said. "But a great storyteller."

Vita couldn't refute this, even if she didn't agree with what happened to all of them. She did think, though, that maybe the bar should've been a bakery. The bomboloni his grandfather made were delicious.

legend

name
> (dates)
>
> nationality
>
> profession/s

title of work
> **syncretisms with close to elsewhere**

Tomas Tranströmer
> (1931 – 2015)
>
> Swedish
>
> Poet
> Psychologist
> Translator

Friends, You Drank Some Darkness (1975):
> **I – the process of bringing one's pieces into play**

Bright Scythe (2015):
> **XXXVII – a large lake and a source of water**
>
> **LVI – italian**
>
> **LVII – indulging in recollection and recreation**

Mario Puzo
> (1920 – 1999)
>
> American
>
> Author
> Screenwriter
> Journalist

The Fortunate Pilgrim (1997):
> **IX – an alcoholic drink taken before a meal to stimulate the appetite**
>
> **XXXV – playing with electrons**
>
> **LXXXII – in attempt to form a spoken or written account of connected events**
>
> **XL – vigor of expression**

Vilhelm Moberg
(1898 – 1973)

Swedish

Journalist
Novelist
Historian
Debater

The Emigrants (1995 Reprint):

XXII – danger

XXIII – a preliminary part, as of a book, musical composition, or the like, leading up to the main part

L – dipped into melting

LI – in relation

LII – with scales that open

LIII – to adapt to the prevailing levels of senses

LXIX – not just sounds, but others

XV – a seat for several people

Melania Mazzucco
(1966 –)

Italian

Novelist
Essayist
Translator

Vita (2006):

XII – late 17th century (originally in the sense 'shake, toss'): from Middle Dutch *hutselen*. Sense 3 of the verb dates from the early 20th century

XXXIV – the practice of growing a series of dissimilar or different types of cultures in the same area in sequenced seasons

XLVI – the study of the way meanings have changed throughout history, e.g. late Middle English from Old French *fantasie* from Latin *phantasia* from Greek 'imagination, appearance'

Selma Lagerlöf
(1858 – 1940)

Swedish

Author
Teacher

Jerusalem (1914):
> XXXVIII – a place of residence;
> a family or family lineage

The Wonderful Adventure
of Nils (1907):
> XlI – sleep lightly / briefly
> XLII – a journey for pleasure
> XLIII – the frigid season

Jhumpa Lahiri
(1967 –)

American

Author
Couragist

Rice (2009 piece from
The New Yorker):
> XLIX – an Indic language of
> West Boston

Stig Dagerman
(1923 – 1954)

Swedish

Journalist
Writer

Sleet (2013 Reprint):
LIV – olive oil

William Carlos Williams
(1883 – 1963)

American

Poet
Physician

The Collected Poems: Volume I, 1909-1939 (1986):
XXVIII – categorisations
LVII – indulging in recollection and recreation
LXXXVIII – an elaborate figuration

Brad McQuaid
(19`` –)

American

Video Game Designer

EverQuest (1999 release):

XXVIII – categorisations

V – (in paleoclimatology) a period of time marked by a characteristic climate

XV – a seat for several people

XXXV – playing with electrons

XXXVII – a large lake and a source of water

LI – in relation

LIII – to adapt to the prevailing level of senses

LIX – rebeginning

LXIII – caused by high temperature

LXIV – like a gate, or other entrance, particularly elaborate

LXXXI – a brief respite of temperatures like this, at night

LXXXV – a supernatural (mis)representation

glossary of experimental language

abbreviations

adj.	adjective
c.	concept
n.	noun
v.	verb
n.f.	novel fragment
p.f.	poem fragment
s.s.f.	short story fragment
v.g.f.	videogame fragment

alcaic (n. p.f.) An alcaic is a Greek lyrical meter experimented within the book, and the title of one of Tomas Tranströmer's poems:

This forest in May. It haunts my whole life: / the invisible moving van. Singing birds. / In silent pools, mosquito larvae's / furiously dancing question marks. / I escape to the same places and same words. / Cold breeze from the sea, the ice-dragon's licking / the back of my neck while the sun glares. / The moving van is burning with cool flames.
Bright Scythe (113)

Poetry collides with prose because the two should coexist.

andaj (c. v. s.s.f.) Elisa takes inspiration from Jhumpa Lahiri's father:

He has a reputation for andaj—the Bengali word for "estimate"— accurately gauging quantities that tend to baffle other cooks. An oracle of rice, if you will. / When my son and daughter were infants, and we celebrated their annaprasans, we hired a caterer, but my father made the pulao, preparing it at home in Rhode Island and transporting it in the trunk of his car to Brooklyn. But by 2005, when it was my daughter's turn, the representative on duty would not permit my father to use the oven, telling him that he was not a licensed cook. My father transferred the pulao from his aluminum trays into glass baking dishes, and microwaved, batch by batch, rice that fed almost a hundred people. When I asked my father to describe that experience, he expressed no frustration. 'It was fine,' he said. 'It was a big microwave.'
Rice (1-3)

Lahiri's father improvises with grace. Elisa adds joy.

155

bouillon cube (c. n. p.f.) A little piece of food in Tranströmer's imagery dips itself into Elisa's family's mind.

I DET FRIA / 1 / Senhöstlabyrint / Vid skogens ingång en bortkastad tomflaska. / Gå in. Skogen är tysta övergivna lokaler så här års. / Bara några få slags ljud: som om någon flyttade kvistar/ försiktigt med en pincett / eller ett gångjärn som gnyr svagt inne i en tjock stam. / Frosten har andats på svamparna och de har skrumpnat. / De liknar föremål och plagg som hittas efter försvunna. / Nu kommer skymningen. Det gäller att hinna ut / och återse sina riktmärken: det rostiga redskapet ute / på åkern / och huset på andra sidan sjön, en rödbrun fyrkant stark /som en buljongtärning.

OUT IN THE OPEN / 1 / Late autumn labyrinth. / On the porch of the woods a thrown-away bottle. / Go in. Woods are silent abandoned houses this time / of year. / Just a few sounds now: as if someone were moving / twigs around carefully with pincers / or as if an iron hinge were whining feebly inside a / thick trunk. / Frost has breathed on the mushrooms and they have shrivelled up. / They look like objects and clothing left behind by people / who've disappeared. / The dusk here already. The thing to do now is to get out / and find the landmarks again: the rusty machine out / in the field / and the house on the other side of the lake, a reddish /square intense as a bullion cube.
Friends, You Drank Some Darkness (214-5)

brännvin (n. n.f.) Literally "burn[t] wine." Brännvin is the Swedish term for a liquor distilled from potatoes or grain. It's everpresent in Moberg's novel, and cameos in the pinecone's cooking.

The peasants ate food which they had brought along and drank brännvin with it, and one of them gave Robert a slice of bread and dram. He dunked the bread in the brännvin as children were wont to do, and he was a little conscious of this, now that he was almost grown.
The Emigrants (26)

dead man floating (n. v.g.f.) EverQuest is an online video game with clerics, wizards, rogues, bards - and necromancers. One of their spells allows levitation and breath without air:

Spell: Dead Man Floating
MAGIC ITEM
Charges: 1
Skill: Abjuration
Mana Cost: 150
Effect: Dead Man Floating
WT: 0.1 Size: SMALL
Class: NEC
Race: ALL

Incorporating EverQuest into the texture of Luca's sense of self lets simulation into real environments. The boundaries of play loosen.

family tree (c.)
MONTALE Vita (née 1935) m. MACAL Joel (né 1930)

MONTALE Elisa (née 1960) m. KEIGHLEY Kirk (né 1962)

KEIGHLEY Luca (né 1995)

fantasy (n. n.f.) Lagerlöf's second text chosen is *The Wonderful Adventures of Nils*. It is fantasy alongside realism.

"What kind of big, checked cloth is this, that I'm looking down on?" said the boy to himself without expecting anyone to answer him. / But instantly, the wild geese who circled around him, called out: "Fields and meadows. Fields and meadows. // Then he understood that the big, checked cloth he was travelling over was the flat land of southern Sweden; and he began to comprehend why it looked so checked and multi colored. The bright green checks he recognized first, they were rye-fields that had been sown in the fall, and had kept themselves green under the winter snows. The yellowish-gray checks were stubble-fields — the remains of the oat- crop which had grown there the summer before. // There were also dark checks with gray centres: these were the large, built-up estates encircled by the small cottages with their blackening straw roofs and their stone-divided landplots. // The boy could not keep from laughing when he saw how checked everything looked."
The Wonderful Adventures of Nils (26)

But as [the elf] walked toward the table, he noticed something remarkable. It couldn't be possible that the cottage had grown. But why was he obliged to take so many more steps than usual to get to the table? And what was the matter with the chair? It looked no bigger than it did a while ago.
The Wonderful Adventures of Nils (6-10; 10-40)

imagine+ (c. v. n.f.) A technique that collages the historical (nonfiction) and the present (fiction, Bookman's extrapolation) to create fiction+, that is, new fiction that is the combination of nonfiction and fiction.

Vita of close to elsewhere is not the Vita of Mazzucco's novel. Nevertheless, her and some of Bookman's characters still have the integrity of her immigrants: between truths and myths of different countries and different continents:

In April 1930, Diamante, age twelve, and Vita, age nine, are sent by their poor families in southern Italy to make a life of themselves in America. // In Vita, the author, Melania G. Mazzucco, also tells her own story of how she found Diamante and Vita in old photographs, documents, ship manifests, and the fading memories of her relatives, and from these fragments of the past imagined this gripping epic fiction of her family's history.
Vita (back cover)

e.g. Vita (historical nonfiction person) + Vita (fictional character) = Mazzucco's novel Vita

Vita (Mazzucco's novel) + Vita reimagined/refictionalized (close to elsewhere)
= fiction+, or imagine+

immersion (n. n.f.) In astronomy, the disappearance of a celestial body in the shadow of or behind another

> *As they talked further he was amazed to learn how little Danjel knew about America; the farmer from Kärragärde was only familiar with the word "America," he knew only that it was the name of another continent, he had not heard of the United States, did not even know where the continent was situated. He knew nothing of its people, government, climate, agriculture, or means of livelihood.*

The Emigrants (139)

Adventure and travel is part-unknown, part-celestial immersion. One never gets to sense the totality of an environment until stepping off the boat, or plane, from the shadows of one's previous conceptions.

intertextual (adj. n.f.) Begun in Sweden and completed in California, the first volume of the Emigrant Novels appeared in 1949 with the Swedish title Utvandrarna. It was published in English in 1951 as The Emigrants.

Nineteenth-century Swedish emigration to America took place in three principal phases: individual, group, and mass migration. Group emigration was most common between 1845 and 1865 as powerful forces, so-called push factors, led many commoners to abandon Sweden. Typical push factors were famine and religious persecution. Most group migration consisted of from fifteen to two hundred people who banded together to start farming or religious settlements in America. / Moberg's first words say that The Emigrants is the tale of such one group. Aside from their general dissatisfaction, the individuals in this group have little in common, however. Instead each person is motivated by a different push factor: crop failure, persecution by the civil

authorities, religious dissent, personal problems, social ostracism, and unfair employment practices.
The Emigrants (xxi)

Part of this text is excerpted from Vilhelm Moberg's historical novel, characters themselves related in what they're reading and how they rearrange themselves in reaction to other fiction and forces of nature.

a Jerusalem of nature (c. n. n.t.)
Transcendentalism, ish.

Two texts by Selma Lagerlöf become incorporated. The first is Jerusalem, a tale of immigration to a promise land. What is curious is tying home not to property, like a city or country, but to a forest: to nature.

"But if young Ingmar seemed to be happy and content, the same could not be said of Strong Ingmar. The old man had of late become sullen and taciturn and difficult to get on with. // I believe you are homesick for the forest,' Ingmar said to him one afternoon as they sat on separate logs eating their sandwiches.'
Jerusalem (172)

olfaction (n. n.f.) specialised sensory receptor cells that form the sense of smell, used to detect hazards, pheromones, and food.

Early the next morning the three wagons drove into Karlshamn and came to a stop near the harbor. A shop clerk with a long birch broom was sweeping the steps in front of a house with the sign Sunesons Skeppshandel. In the air was the odor of fish, tar, hemp, herring, salt, and sea.
The Emigrants (192)

It's said that for people whose diets have never included dairy, Irish people smell like milk. For those not from Karlshamn, or Cape Cod, fishing villages (and people) smell, too. Any environment (or people) smells - differently - if one has never lived in that environment before!

olive oil (n. s.s.f.) Olive oil is adapted from one of Stig Dagerman's stories, Snöblandat regn. A Swedish boy's aunt visits from America, causing much confusion.

I'll never forget this day when we were chopping carrots, when it was raining and the rain turned to sleet, and when the aunt from America was coming here to stay. // [...] // 'Por liddel boi,' says the aunt from America, whatever that means, as she pulls me up tight against her. // [...] // She strokes her little soft hand across my face. // 'Are you crying?' she says. // 'No,' I say, and I dry and dry till the carrot-tops glisten green again, all freshly cut in

the lamplight. '... It's just a little sleet.'
Sleet (51-60)

It is now Luca the American boy who is confused. His aunt visits from Italy, some Swedish sentiments now within him.

money (c. n. n.f.)
Money was a new homeland. Lying awake at night thinking of the growing sums in the bank, Lucia Santa felt the sudden physical chilling sharpness mixed with fear that a prisoner feels when counting the days to stay behind walls.
The Fortunate Pilgrim (86)

Obsessing about money is not Thomi's preferred state. He - and on some level Lucia Santa, other characters - would rather think about joie de vivre (joy of living), sometimes forgotten in a pragmatic orientation of wealth.

simultaneity (n. p.f.) At the same time; the whole series of past events connected. Tranströmer's imagery is of many states, rendering one place another simultaneously.

ÖSTERSJÖAR/ Vinden går i tallskogen. Det susar /tungt och lätt. / Östersjön susar också mitt inne på ön, / långt inne i skogen är man ute på öppna sjön.

BALTICS / (Wind enters the pine forest. It sighs / heavily and lightly. // Likewise the Baltic sighs in the /island's interior; deep in the forest / you're out on the open sea)
Bright Scythe (46-7).

sunrise (n. p.f.) Tranströmer drifts; his imagery creates paradox. The following poem's movement suffuses heat over endpoints, turning Luca's pragmatic attitudes towards vacation.

KVÄLL--MORGON / Ut på trappan. Gryningen slår och slår i / havets gråstensgrindar och solen sprakar / nära världen. Halvkvävda sommargudar famlar i sjörök.

EVENING--MORNING / Out on the stoop. The sunrise is / opening and slamming / granite gates of the ocean and the sun sparkles / near the world. Half-suffocated summer gods grope / in the seasmoke.
Friends, You Drank Some Darkness (173)

stone (n. n.f.) Stone can be beautiful, unless stone was the material that imprisoned. In Sweden it was a heavy reminder of being locked into a socio-economic class.

[Karl Oskar] went out to inspect the unbroken ground belonging to

Korpamoen. There were spruce woods and knolls, there were desolate sandy plains with juniper and pine roots, there were low swamplands with moss and cranberries, there were hillocks and tussock-filled meadows. The rest was strewn with stone. He carried an iron bar which he now and then stuck into the ground, and always he heard the same sound: stone. he went through pastures and meadows, through woodlands and moors, and everywhere the same sound: stone, stone, stone. It was a monotonous tune, a sad tune for a man who wanted to clear more acres.
The Emigrants (12)

style hybridisation (c. v. p.f.) An attempt to stylize Tranströmer with William Carlos Williams. Both a doctor and a writer, Williams' sweet apologetic nature is hybrid, both clinical and innocent.

I have eaten / the plums / that were in / the icebox // and which / you were probably / saving / for breakfast / Forgive me / they were delicious / so sweet / and so cold
This Is Just To Say, The Collected Poems: Volume I, 1909-1939

temper (c. v. n.f.) Adjusting note intervals; improving elasticity by heating then cooling.

The beginnings of the novel Vita. The retracing of unknown friends, relatives, the unfamiliarity of old places — incorporated into Luca's family, but tempered with Lagerlöfian fantasy:

Everyone is old here. Where have the children gone who used to play in the streets? 'Where is Via San Leonardo?' he asks the old man, forcing himself to dig up a bit of the language they have in common. 'My son,' she responds with a toothless smile, 'this is it.'
Vita (5)

transmogrify (v.)
Mrs. Colucci spoke a refined Italian she could never have learned in Italy. They were not the children of mountain presents but from the class of officials, of long generations of civil servants in Italy.
The Fortunate Pilgrim (92)

Luca is a Colucci of sorts. Mrs. Colluci had learned a chiseled Italian from childhood, in Italy, whereas Luca was on the way to studying a new Italian, still in America. It's the effect of fascism and acculturation in historical tango, where the disappearance of many Italian dialects revive themselves in the bodies of fourth and fifth-generation Americans.

vestigial (c. adj. n.f.) Reduced or functionless in the course of evolution. The vestiges of European digestif culture hazes over Puzo's novel:

"Guido served coffee and filled the stranger's anisette glass."
The Fortunate Pilgrim (187)

Offered to a stranger, a glass of anisette serves as scaffolding. Luca, too, tests this in a new environment: among Internet friends.

will-o'-the-wisp (c. n. n.f.) Incorporating the folklore of the will-o'-the-wisp, which is the difficulty of capturing magic, or thought of in the context of immigration, believing in the faith of a new journey from Sweden to America, apparent in any faith of seeing what you can't see:

There was much talk in this village about this strange projected undertaking […] how could he relinquish his farm, the parental home whose deed he had, and reach out for land in faraway North America, a country which neither he nor anyone else had seen? Wasn't it like trying to catch the will-o'-the-wisp on a misty morning?
The Emigrants (127)

The challenge is to capture one's own magic in spite of ecological or cultural forces that inhibit or shame radical adventures of the imagination.

Will-o'-the-wisps also appeared in the early days of EverQuest. Simulations of nature flicker amongst picaresque adventure as a way to assist the imagination. These characters respect a divinity of all senses necessary for their evolution.

acknowledgments

Sofi Tegsveden Deveaux the Beliefist.
Andy Bolton, the tinkerer.
Amanda Stojanov, media artist and educator.
Brian Tholl and Eleonora Sartoni, Italian scholars at Pennsylvania State University
and Rutgers University: exceptional knowledge, exceptional sensitivity.

Carel, Rob, Ward, Niko, all those taught at Wightman Tennis Center.
Door No. 7 - one-part Brazilian tongs and a chef's cut, ¡many-parts crudo!
the people I've played with on EverQuest.

småkaka, my first Swedish friend
my Italian friends and family from Crema,
an Alba jacket, a blessèd wedding, a gnocchi feast. Anna, Marco, the poetry is all of you the French goodmother, la magicienne des confitures my teachers from high school, Brandeis, ArtCenter, the Middlebury Italian School, Syracuse University in Florence

Alliance Française.
namesake_beauty, the first light in the morning.
Hau, Jade, Justin, Julia, Selina, magic accelerators.
Nan the Violining Willowisp.
Mariah, the parks in our heads.

Christine and the Reines, the Alexes, the Jasons, Mareshia, James, Alonzo, Alice, Yashar, Hedda, Leila, Karen, Darlene, Phoebe, jetdi, gg, adventures and formation sans s.v.p.
the Paymans, the Oftadehs, the Solano-Joelles, dingue coffee, wood racquets, and nan-e nokhodchi, the Dirrens, the Mazzellas, the Adu-Gyamfis, for chaletesque traces of laughter and support, for your positive energies. It keeps me moving.

Hannah, Lee and Lizzie, for your kind eyes, Harriet and Marlene Reis, for your devotion, Mike and Alissa.

For my parents.

about the author
joshua kent bookman

Joshua Kent Bookman (1990) is an American performer and writer, born and living in Boston, Massachusetts. Taste, smell, and emotion play a central role in his works and his environments, helping him syncretize moments and reflections from real and imaginary places. He considers such syncretization a tool in order to voice ideas between cultures.

Bookman is devoted to multicultural education, and views his writing as an extension of multisensory communication — moments of taste, touch, and smell, however brief, however foreign to inherited ways of seeing, hearing, and thinking. His writing also reflects his experience of living and working in France and Italy, his adventures elsewhere, and the various jobs he has tried — agricultural laborer, high school teacher, and tennis instructor. Emphasis on tried.

He is also a devoted traveler and language learner, and has studied languages at the Middlebury College Italian School, Syracuse University in Florence, and Alliance Française in Bordeaux. He holds a B.A. from Brandeis University and M.F.A. from ArtCenter.

close to elsewhere is Bookman's first novel.

Printed in Poland
by Amazon Fulfillment
Poland Sp. z o.o., Wrocław